SOMETIMES YOU JUST KILL THE WRONG PEOPLE

AND OTHER STORIES

GILES EKINS

Copyright (C) 2021 Giles Ekins

Layout design and Copyright (C) 2021 by Next Chapter

Published 2021 by Next Chapter

Edited by Fading Street Services

Cover art by CoverMint

Back cover texture by David M. Schrader, used under license from Shutterstock.com

Mass Market Paperback Edition

This book is a work of fiction. Names, characters, places, and incidents are the product of the author's imagination or are used fictitiously. Any resemblance to actual events, locales, or persons, living or dead, is purely coincidental.

All rights reserved. No part of this book may be reproduced or transmitted in any form or by any means, electronic or mechanical, including photocopying, recording, or by any information storage and retrieval system, without the author's permission.

*For Patricia, who told me for many years to get my
short stories published as a book.
So, here is the first volume.
XXX*

AUTHORS NOTE

Some of these stories have appeared in magazines, anthologies or in larger works but adapted here for the short story format. A few were written many years ago, and it shows.

SOMETIMES YOU JUST KILL THE WRONG PEOPLE

Sometimes you just kill the wrong people.

There are errors, mistakes, major errors, bad mistakes, and fatal errors and when Jason Jordan Smith murdered Angelina Lucia La Malfa he made a mistake of catastrophic proportions.

Now there is no denying that Jason Jordan Smith was an extreme psychopath compelled by the darkest of urges of torture and murder. He was a sadist, a twisted and tormented mass murderer who tortured his victims before slowly strangling them and by dint of good fortune he remained undetected for more than a dozen years as he toured the countryside with his mobile torture chamber but even so, he really should have been more careful about the choice of his last victim.

Jason was a loner who never knew his father. There was no father named on his birth certificate, and his mother, a consultant paediatrician at a local hospital, refused to answer any questions about his father or who had fathered him. He hated his mother for that. In fact, he hated his mother for just about everything. He also hated the remainder of the human race. At school Jason was an above average pupil, not outstanding but was good enough to pass his GCSEs in nine subjects, achieving his best marks in maths and chemistry. He was quiet in class, somewhat of a loner, and the other kids, especially the girls, thought him a bit creepy. Whilst other adolescent boys might fantasise about sex with a pin-up girl or the prettiest girl in class, Jason's fantasies were far darker, fierier, and filled with flames and agony and screams.

Like most psychopaths, Jason Jordan Smith started early in life, when he was twelve years old, Lucy, the family cat produced a kindle of unwanted kittens However, instead of taking the kittens to a vet to be humanely put down as his mother instructed, he took the tiny beasts out into the woods behind his house and tortured them, holding them by the tail, head first over a lighted candle, revelling as the kittens squealed in agony as he roasted their heads, imitating the torture that Apache Indians and other Indian tribes inflicted on their captives, suspending them head first over a slow fire so that their blackened roasting skulls finally cracked and split after hours of agony.

The last of the kittens he impaled on a stick and then left it to die in agony. The other bodies he tossed deep into the woodland where the foxes and crows would soon find them and so destroy the evidence. The feeling of sublime ecstasy, of exhilaration that Jason felt as he inflicted the torments was so overwhelmingly powerful, he knew, from that point in time, the road that he would be travelling. He was destined to be a sadist, a torture-inflicting murderer, he knew this with such clarity it was a blinding light of revelation. Some people feel a calling to the church, Jason felt a calling to torture and murder.

Following the torture of the kittens, his next formative atrocity, apart from pulling the wings of flies and crisping butterflies over candles, saw Jason capturing the toy poodle belonging to a neighbour, taping its jaws together to stop it barking. He then took the struggling dog deep into the woods where he spitted the beast and roasted it alive over a fire, ejaculating in ecstasy as the tortured beast screamed out its torment in muffled squeals and agonised yelps. He was fourteen years old.

At other times he bought white mice, rats, guinea pigs, or hamsters from local pet shops and also tortured them to death by fire, always by fire. He loved fire, worshipped the flames, loved the pain of fire, loved the pain it inflicted, and all his tortures involved the agony of fire. Often, he would simply burn himself. Simply for the agony and the ecstasy of fire.

He was fascinated with torture by fire. His favourite readings were accounts of Comanche and Apache tortures, his favourite picture an engraving of the death of Col. William Crawford, tortured to death by Shawnee Indians during the Indian wars following American Independence. Crawford was staked to the ground and a fire laid across his stomach, his agonies so clearly etched you could almost hear his screams whilst another captive looks on in horror, aghast at the fate which awaited him also. Crawford was then burned alive at the stake in a slow fire. Every time Jason looked at this picture, in an illustrated book about the Indian wars, he felt a frisson of excitement surge through his groin. One day, he avowed to himself, he would do the same.

When he was eighteen, his hated mother Alison died in circumstances that have never been satisfactorily explained. There was a house fire in which she died from smoke inhalation and although the police and fire brigade suspected arson nothing could be proven, no trace of accelerants were found, no signs of petrol or paraffin or any other inflammables and consequently the cause of the fire was given as an overloaded extension lead with fourteen appliances attached to it, but DI Stanley Morgan was never satisfied with this explanation but could find nothing to indicate Jason's involvement in the fire, but his copper's instinct told him otherwise. He was convinced that Jason Jordan Smith had somehow caused the fire which killed his mother.

'It just does not smell right, I've got this prickling at the back of my neck that tells me that somehow, that boy had something to do with that fire, don't ask me how. Or why. I just know it.'

But the only suspicious circumstance that the autopsy revealed was that Alison Smith had ingested enough sleeping tablets to render her unconscious for hours and so would not have been aware of the fire which killed her. Sleeping tablets which she had purloined from the hospital dispensary.

After her funeral, Jason duly claimed on his mother's life insurances. She had two policies, one of which only recently taken out, then there were the house and contents insurances and although the insurers shared the same disquiet about the cause of the fire, they had no option but to settle and in addition Jason discovered that his unknown, unnamed father had been paying a substantial maintenance allowance for Jason, most of which his mother had put aside for his university fees and with other extensive savings she had made from her job as a paediatric consultant, Jason Jordan Smith suddenly found himself to be a very wealthy young man.

He soon came to realise that he now had the means

to fulfil all his darkest fantasies, the means to buy a secluded house with deep cellars far away from prying eyes, far enough away so that screams could not be heard, and not wishing to draw too much attention to himself, he bought a second-hand Ford Transit van and fitted it out as a mobile torture chamber, soundproofing the walls and fitting shackles and handcuffs to suspend his victims from the van roof. However, he was careful to only ever take his torture-mobile out at night and only on those nights when he was actively hunting for his prey. The rest of the time he drove a nondescript six-year-old Volkswagen Passat.

He enrolled at university in Sheffield, the city where he lived, to study to be a maths teacher, so that he could disappear behind a cloak of respectability, but he soon dropped out as other, more urgent issues began to press down upon him – the need to kill. The burning need to kill and torture.

Apart from his first victims, Jason Jordan Smith never took victims from his hometown, he was far too cautious for that. He picked up what was possibly his second victim (if indeed he did start the fire that killed his mother) from outside a gay club in Sheffield. Not that Jordan was gay, there again he was not heterosexual either, if anything at all he was asexual with absolutely no interest in sex. He got his thrills in other ways and his female victims were never raped or sexually assaulted in any way. And neither were the males (except in cases where their genitals were burned off).

It was raining heavily as Anthony Swallowfield, a nineteen-year-old Philosophy student left the Pink Rabbit club. It was after midnight, the buses had stopped running, and he had no money left to pay for a taxi, having spent far more than he should have at the club—the drinks were so expensive and a snort or two of cocaine he bought in the toilets from a dealer also drained his money and although his allowance from his father was generous, he could not afford to squander his money like this. He was not actually sure if he was gay. He was still exploring his sexuality and although he had received two offers from older men to spend the night with them, he had declined, not quite ready to take that step although now soaking wet in the rain he wished that he had taken up at least one offer. It was going to be a long, cold, and wet walk back to his digs.

A blue Volkswagen Passat drew up alongside him. 'Hi mate, you look a bit wet, you want a lift somewhere?' Jason Jordan Smith called to him as he wound down the window, giving Anthony a disarming smile. The coke and booze had deadened Anthony's sense of caution and he accepted with alacrity. 'Yeah, thanks, I'm a bit wet though, on your seats I mean.'

'No worries.'

'Great!' Anthony got into the car. After some mundane chat about the weather and university life and some detail about Anthony and his life, Jason asked him if he wanted to go back to his house and 'dry out.' Anthony accepted and lay back in his seat as the booze and coke buzzed around his head.

Jason ushered Anthony into his house—the first guest he ever had—gave him a towel to dry off and made him a cup of coffee, after which Anthony fell asleep, drugged by Alison Smith's purloined sleeping tablets. He awoke to find himself spreadeagled on the floor of the cellar. He was naked and shackled by the wrist and ankles. A wood fire blazed nearby, casting lurid shadows on the whitewashed walls as Jason walked around him, savouring the moment when his wildest fantasy would come to fulfilment.

'Hey, man,' Anthony shouted, suddenly very afraid, 'I don't do bondage, not into that BDSM shit. No way. Let me up, let me go. Please. Please.'

With responding or saying a word, Jason picked up a glowing orange red ember with a pair of barbecue tongs and carefully laid it on Anthony's stomach. The screams echoed and echoed and echoed around the cellar. It was a long time before he finally expired. Jason's exhilaration was intense, during the torture session he had ejaculated, and he was on the highest of highs, far higher than any of Anthony's cocaine induced highs.

Anthony Swallowfield's body was never recovered. In the dark of the following night, Jason loaded it into back of the Transit and buried it in an isolated wooded copse somewhere several miles away on the moors of the Peak District. It is not known precisely how many others Jason tortured and killed but it is believed that at least thirteen victims, mostly girls, fell into his clutches, to be either taken back to the cellars in his Sheffield house or tortured to death in the van and then disposed of. Some bodies were never recovered and some were simply dumped in lonely stretches of road. He travelled all over the north of England in search of his prey, Bradford, Salford, Harrogate, Doncaster, Bury, Derby, Ripon, and Glossop amongst other localities.

The police were eventually aware that a serial killer who tortured and burned his victims was at large, operating throughout the region, but despite intensive cooperation between forces and eventually the setting up of a dedicated team, no progress was made in apprehending the most notorious killer of the age. Even the sighting of a ubiquitous white Transit van in areas where victims had disappeared brought police no nearer finding the killer. There are thousands of such vehicles on the roads, and Jason either fitted stolen number plates or obscured the plates with mud whenever he was on the prowl. Who knows how long he might have continued burning and killing his way across the country if he had not murdered Angelina Lucia La Malfa?

However, it was that killing that brought about his downfall. Angelina was the only daughter of Don Luciano Alessandro La Malfa, a prominent Sicilian man of business. Don Luciano and his wife Elena had six sons besides Angelina, but she was the baby of the family, conceived years after Elena thought her childbearing days were over, and Don Luciano doted on her. He could not refuse her anything and when, at eighteen years old she begged to leave Sicily and study overseas, despite the concerns of every father when a beloved daughter wishes to go away to study, he could not refuse. Angelina wanted to go to England, to study but also to travel the country, to visit the famous sights. Don Luciano preferred that she study in the US where there were extensive family connections who could keep an eye and look out for her but Elena, his wife, did not agree.

'America, it is not safe for a young girl. In England she will be much safer.' And reluctantly Don Luciano agreed. So, Angelina duly enrolled at the University of York to study Italian and Linguistics. It was during the second term of her second years that she disappeared. Her brutalised burned body was recovered some thirty-five miles away from York on Helmsley Moors above the A171 on the way to the east coast.

'You told me she would be safe in England,' Don

Luciano railed at his wife as they flew from Palermo to repatriate her body for internment in the family vault in the grounds of their villa on the outskirts of Messina, but Elena made no response, knowing that Luciano was only expressing his grief, that he did not in truth blame her for their daughter's death.

When Don Luciano viewed Angelina's tortured body as she lay in the mortuary, his grief and anger knew no bounds. He knelt beside her and took her charred hand in his.

'I swear my Angelina, my beautiful angel, I swear by all that I hold dear in this life, I swear on my life that I shall avenge you. I swear that whoever has done this shall suffer as no man has ever suffered before, to this, my angel I vow and dedicate my life. I will find the man who did this. I will find him and destroy him.'

He listened out of courtesy to the platitudes of the police leading the investigation, but he had little faith that they would find his daughter's killer and bring him to justice, but in any case, he did not seek justice, he sought vengeance. What else can a man, a father, a Sicilian do but seek retribution?

Don Luciano was not a man to take his problems to the police for was not only was he a respected man of business, but he was a man of respect, the head of the secretive but very powerful Sciascia crime family, even the more widely known Cosa Nostra clans such as the Navarra, Cascioferro, and La Barbera clans owed allegiance to the Sciascia. The tentacles of the Sciascia spread far and wide, far beyond the boundaries of Sicily or mainland Italy and the resources at his disposal far outweighed that of any policeman or police force.

A week after the funeral of Angelina, Don Luciano drove up into the hills above his villa and after parking his car in a secluded glade, made his way into a deep cave, the entrance well hidden by thick bush amongst the towering crags and rocks, walking deeper and deeper into the cave until it opened out into a vast cavern. At the far end of the cavern stood a black basalt altar on which stood two black candles. Don Luciano prostrated himself before the altar for not only was he the most powerful capo di tutti capo, the boss of bosses of Sicilian mafia, he was also Grand Master of the Order of Cagliostro, an even more secretive society, dedicated to the Black Arts and the service of Satan and especially the Satanic Grand Duke Astorath.

After his obeisance to his infernal master, Don Luciano made his plea and subsequently entered into a Demonic Pact. Firstly, a sacrifice must be made and the next day Don Luciano sacrificed five-year-old Luigi Camilleri, the son of a peasant farmer, on the black basalt altar, slitting his throat with a long curved knife, collecting blood in a silver chalice and drinking it. On his return to the temple four days later, he was given the name of Jason Jordan Smith as the killer of his daughter Angelina. Another sacrifice was due and nineteen-year-old Margaret Riccobono a student the same age as Angelina, who was studying at the University of Catania was slain on the profane altar in payment for what was to come.

The next day Don Luciano La Malfa flew to Heathrow and after an overnight stay in London caught the train to Sheffield.

Jason Jordan Smith's fate now awaited him. Irrevocable, inevitable, and Inexorable.

It was the cold that awoke him, such intense cold that seeped into bones and flesh, his breath billowing in clouds before of his face. He shivered deeper into his bedding, but the iciness grew. His teeth chattered uncontrollably in the gelid night air. The darkness about him seemed to intensify, a darker blacker nightdark, as if all light in the room had leached out, and the darkness was palpable and solid, as if he could reach out and touch it, as if it had tangible substance.

Then the baleful yellow eyes glared out of the blackness and he gave out an involuntary scream, biting his tongue as his teeth continued to violently chatter. He could taste the bitter saltiness of his blood on his tongue, and he swallowed down, his gorge rising. He suddenly felt very, very afraid. From the far side of his bedroom, he heard a voice, a voice redolent with hatred, avid for vengeance.

'Tu sei il mostro che hanno bruciatola mia bella figlia, ora faro bruciare, bruciare fino alla fine del tempo.' (You are the monster who burned my beautiful daughter, now I shall burn you, burn you to the end of time).

'What the… who… who the fuck are you and what do you want?' Jason managed to croak. Suddenly the room burst into blinding light, an explosion of light, a dazzling, blinding, fearsome radiance that seared into his eyeballs, darts of agony spearing into his skull. He screamed again, not in fear but in pain, a pain that threatened to explode his head. He clutched at his temples as his wretched screams echoed around the walls, such agony he had never felt, such agony he could never have imagined.

'Stop it, stop it, please I beg you, whatever it is, laser, please stop it.'

'Qui mihi amicus est initium operationis tuæ tormenta' (That, my friend is but the beginnings of your torment)

As suddenly it had begun, the agony in his eyeballs subsided although the bright light in the room remained.

'Thank you, thank you' he gasped, holding his head in his hands as the last of the pain ebbed away. 'What do you want? he asked again, 'I don't keep money in the house but take anything else you want, only please don't hurt me again.'

'You are Jason Jordan Smith?' the voice spoke again, this time in accented English.

'Yeah, yeah, what of it?'

'Look up. Look up at me Jason Jordan Smith. Look at me.'

Slowly Jason raised his head and gave a start of horror. Before him stood a tall, olive-skinned man of an indeterminate age, sixty to sixty-five years old, immaculately dressed in a well-cut grey suit, white shirt, red tie, and highly polished shoes but it was the creature next to him that sent the shivers of fear down his spine. It was a creature from Hell, a vision of absolute evil, horned, bat-winged, with skin of shimmering blood red scales, glaring, flaring yellow eyes, a fanged mouth emitting fetid breath, reptilian claws, and hoofed feet, it was a fiend beyond human imagining, a fell beast of such hideousness that even the gargoyles of Notre Dame could not match.

'I am Don Luciano La Malfa and you, you burned my daughter Angelina, you took my only precious jewel. Now you will pay.'

'Pay?' A surge of hope flared through Jason, if this was just about payment, about blood money he might yet get out of his situation. Whatever the hell this situation was. 'I can pay, I have money, 'he burbled.

'Money? You think this is about money? That I

want money? You insult me, Jason Jordan Smith. You will pay for Angelina tenfold, a thousandfold, with pain and agony. You will pay with your soul! Bring him.'

Jason whimpered in terror as the fiendish creature, demon, whatever, dragged him down to the cellar torture chamber. The strength of the monster was enormous, and Jason's resistance was useless as he was hung by his wrists from the roof by his own shackles and pulley. Don Luciano picked up one of Jason's favourite instruments of torture, a kitchen blowtorch, and began to slowly extract his vengeance as the cellar echoed with agonised screams and the stench of burning skin and flesh permeated the very fabric of the walls.

At the end of every extensive torture session, Jason was lowered to the floor, and the demon, using diabolic medical skills kept him alive for more torment. Over the coming days Don Luciano remorselessly burned away every inch of Jason's bodily skin, leaving him a charred blackened hulk, hovering perpetually on the brink of death but never being allowed to die as the demoniac nurse patiently kept the thin flicker of life alive for yet more torture. Whatever Anthony Swallowfield, whatever all his other victims, whatever Angelina Lucia La Malfa had suffered was nothing compared to the agonies meted out by Don Luciano on the agony-wracked being that was all that remained of Jason Jordan Smith. The Don, the man of respect, was devilishly patient, adhering to the Sicilian creed that revenge is a dish best served cold.

Finally Don Luciano's vengeance was all but sated, even the ministrations of the demon could not keep Jason alive much longer. Without such treatment he would have died so much earlier, days earlier but Don

Luciano extracted his vengeance to the utmost and in a final, ironic twist he suspended Jason headfirst over a bed of red hot coals, the Apache torture which Jason so admired and as the life began to slowly bleed away through his blackened cracking roasted skull, Don Luciano bent down to speak to him one last time.

'Jason Jordan Smith, you have paid with your body, now you shall pay with your soul, this creature beside me is the demon Nuberus, gatekeeper to the depths of Hell, when, finally, you die, he will drag you to the fiery pits to burn for eternity. Arrivederci.'

At that, Don Luciano La Malfa got to his feet and left the dying Jason to the less than tender mercies of the demon Nuberus. He had done his duty to his murdered daughter, his duty as a man, as a father and as a Sicilian.

And as I say, as Jason Jordan Smith found to his cost, sometimes you just kill the wrong people.

A DEALER IN FINE ART

Christopher DeVilliers (which might or might not be his real name) walked purposefully across the ground floor lobby and took one of the high-speed elevators serving the upper floors. He carried with him a large brown leather holdall bag and a thin leather attaché case.

Alighting at a floor below his final destination, he walked over to the toilets on the lobby floor and waited until they were empty. He then took a thin, hooked lock pick from his pocket and expertly picked the lock of the janitor store and placed the holdall inside. He had previously monitored the schedule of the cleaners and knew that it would be an hour or more before anyone came to clean.

Closing and locking the door he slipped the lock pick down into his sock where it would not be found in a body search pat down.

He then took the elevator up to the floor above and his appointment with the Vice President of the United Bank of Osaka.

'Good morning,' he said to the Japanese receptionist, 'Christopher DeVilliers, I have an appointment with Mr. Nakazawa,' handing her his business card as he did so. The card was simple, stating only his name and occupation: 'Dealer in Fine Art'.

The girl spoke into her headphone and a minute or so, a massive man, built like a Sumo wrestler, walked powerfully into the reception area. This, DeVilliers knew, was Atsushi Kawaguchi, the Vice President's personal assistant or bodyguard.

Kawaguchi signalled for DeVilliers to raise his arms for a pat down body search, not a normal procedure for an interview with a bank manager, but DeVilliers seemed unfazed. The search was professional and thorough and then Kawaguchi took the attaché case and methodically examined that, checking for a hidden weapon or blade. Finally satisfied, he gave a grunt and gestured for DeVilliers to follow him.

Yoshikatsu Kawazawa stood up from his desk and walked around to greet his visitor, bowing as he did so. DeVilliers gave a slight nod back and the two men shook hands.

'Thank you for seeing me, Nakazawa-san, especially at such short notice.'

'If what you are selling is as you say, I would have cancelled all my appointments regardless how important.'

'You are most gracious, however, before we start, might I just use a washroom?'

'Hei. Of course, please make use of my private facility, here.' And he pointed to a door to the left of him.

Inside the washroom DeVilliers stripped out his belt from the trouser loops, twisted the buckle sharply, and using the buckle as a handle drew out a thin six-inch flexible blade from within the belt. The blade was crafted from a high tensile ceramic material developed for the space industry, undetectable by metal detectors and stronger than steel and honed to an edge as keen as the sharpest Samurai sword.

DeVilliers slipped the blade into a soft chamois sheath tailored into the inside of his jacket and re-joined the Japanese. Opening the attaché case, DeVilliers slipped out an A4 coloured photocopy of a Pablo Picasso painting. 'As discussed, I think this will be of interest, Nakazawa-san,' sliding the picture across the desk to Nakazawa who eagerly took the copy, his eyes darting with delight.

'Picasso's 'Portrait of Dora Maar'. How can this be, this painting is in the National Gallery of Victoria in Melbourne?'

'It was,' DeVilliers answered dryly, 'It has been... how shall we say... liberated? The provenance is genuine and guaranteed.' He passed across a photocopy of an article from the 'Melbourne Herald,' describing the theft of the Picasso,

Whilst Nakazawa and Kawaguchi were distracted with the angular faced portrait of one of Picasso's lovers, DeVilliers slid his knife from its sheath, stepped over behind the giant Kawaguchi, and swiftly slit the bodyguard's throat, jumping back sharply to avoid the sudden spurt of blood. Nakazawa jerked back, reaching for an alarm button, opened his mouth to shout, but was too late, way too late. DeVilliers had seized his hair, jerked back his head, and also slit his throat, the ceramic blade slicing through flesh and bone with ease. Nakazawa fell forward, his head making a loud thump onto the highly polished maple top of his desk, a puddle of blood slickly oozing across a leather-bound blotter.

DeVilliers carefully wiped the blood from his blade, using Nakazawa's Hermes tie to do so before retrieving his belt and slipping the blade back inside.

The United Bank of Osaka was in fact a money-laundering front for the Osaka yakuza, the Japanese mafia, and Nakazawa a high-ranking yakuza officer sent from Japan to control the operation. But then the Osaka yakuza had ordered the assassination of Nakazawa, suspected of laundering money to his own account. Substantial sums could not be accounted for and he now had paid the price.

Christopher DeVilliers (which might or might not be his real name) was one of the world's foremost killers for hire and had been contracted by the Osaka yakuza because a Westerner would be less likely to arouse Nakazawa's suspicions than a Japanese assassin. Nakazawa's indiscreet taste for expensive stolen works of art had been DeVilliers entree to the reclusive and paranoid yakuza banker; the stolen Picasso had been tempting bait.

The actual killing had been easy.

Closing and locking Nakazawa's office door behind him, DeVilliers walked away without haste and bade goodbye to the Japanese receptionist, even glancing up to look at the CCTV security camera as he did so. The Christopher DeVilliers who entered the building would look nothing like the one who left. He smiled to himself as he thought about the business card he had left with the girl, 'Dealer in Fine Art,' absolutely true, a dealer in the fine art of murder.

Retrieving his holdall from the janitor store, he locked himself in a toilet cubicle.

When he emerged, he was wearing a bright blue overall with the name' Project Maintenance' emblazoned across the back, he sported a thick walrus moustache which covered much of his face, had plumped out his cheeks with soft rubber pads and had a 'Project Maintenance' baseball cap pulled down low over his forehead. He carried a yellow, plastic, workman's bag which contained his holdall, briefcase, and jacket.

Whistling tunelessly, he punched the call button on the elevator. Another job well done, another million dollars in the bank. It was the twenty-seventh professional killing of his career, although, of course, there had been many more of a personal nature.

The lift was slow in coming, but he was in no hurry. Just then the building seemed to shake violently as if struck, and a deep crashing noise echoed up the stairwell, a sound the world had never heard before. Dust trickled down from the ceiling. 'Earthquake' was his immediate thought and he jabbed at the call button violently with his thumb, over and over again but the lift floor indicators were not moving.

Realising that the lift was not arriving he crossed over to the emergency staircase. Opening the door, he was met with a blast of heat and smoke. Vicious yellow flame could be seen flickering across the staircase walls, the smoke billowing thick and black.

He felt a spurt of fear clutch at his heart, and he quickly shut the door and ran across to the other stairwell. Workers from the offices were also running to the exit, also to be beaten back here by the smoke and flames. Screams and shouts. A terrified babble of noise echoing around the marble clad walls of the elevator lobby. More and more people crowded, panic rippling through the crushing masses. Forcing his way through the crowd with kicks and curses, DeVilliers forced his way into the stairwell, covered his face to shield from the heat and worked his way upwards. *Get to the roof,* he told himself, *I can be rescued from the roof.*

But a tide of terrified people, fleeing down the stairs, pushed him back unseeing. He lost his grip on the bag, a woman tripped over it and brought several people down with her, screaming as the panicked mob trampled over her.

The fear that clutched his heart and bowels gripped DeVilliers like a clamp, a ruthless killer who had never before in his life ever felt fear.

He forced his way out from the terror-driven stairs and fled into an open office. The heat and choking smoke had now reached these upper levels and he realised that he and hundreds more were trapped by the rising inferno.

He had to get out, he had a flight, First Class of course, to Geneva where he would arrange the transfer of his contract fee to the Cayman Islands and then an onward flight to Rio de Janeiro where his taste for prepubescent boys could be readily satisfied.

The flames and smoke surged through the stairwell doors like a charging bull, rolling through the open plan office in a fiery tidal wave. A woman screamed with terror and threw herself out from an open window, preferring to fall to her death than be burnt alive.

DeVilliers, whimpering in fear, flung himself beneath a desk, coughing as the smoke tendrils curled around to greet him.

Not too long afterwards, the North Tower of the World Trade Centre in New York City, collapsed in upon itself, the tallest building in America being unable to withstand the impact of an airliner deliberately flown into it.

Many remains would later be removed from the

rubble, but of Mr. Christopher DeVilliers (which might or might not have been his real name) no trace was ever found.

AUNT ALICE

'So, you came then,' Uncle Leonard said, standing by the front door of Ravensdale House.

'Evidently, since I'm standing here in front of you,' I answered.

'Ah yes, as I recall, you always did have a smart mouth.'

'And as I recall, the last time we met was when you came to Dad's funeral five years ago. You sat at the back of the church, and afterwards you muttered some meaningless banalities, shook my hand, and cleared off again. You didn't even bother with the reception afterwards, did you?

That's exactly how it was. He was waiting by the door as we filed out and introduced himself as my Uncle Leonard, although for all I knew he could have been my Uncle Zog from the planet Kronos. 'Sorry to hear about Joseph,' he muttered, shook my hand, those of my brother Beanie (real name Benjamin) and his cow-faced wife Alison, strode off, climbed into a gleaming black Rolls Royce, circa 1950 and drove off without out so much as a wave or a glance behind.

'I'm not much of a one for funerals,' Uncle Leonard responded, not at all put out by my rudeness.

'Or families for that matter.'

'Perhaps you're right, but there again look at the family I was stuck with.'

'Didn't make much effort, did you?' I said, determined not to be brow-beaten by him.

'Richard, its cold out there, are you coming inside, or are we going to stay out here all night, bickering like kids in the playground?'

I looked back to where my ten-year-old, sky blue, Saab 9.5 convertible was parked, sorely tempted to climb back in and get out of there. But no, displaying my customary indecisiveness, I meekly followed Uncle Leonard up the short flight of steps and into the house.

'Come on in, leave your bag in the hall, we'll take it up later when I show you to your room.'

Dutifully I dropped my soft-sided suitcase onto the floor and followed him. 'Come into the lounge, or the sitting room, whatever you care to call it. *Parlour?* I thought. *Come into the parlour said the spider to the fly.*

'Parlour?'

'Parlour, oh yes, very good,' he said, obviously picking up the allusion to the spider and the fly. 'Perhaps you did not inherit your father's dim wits after all.'

'Are you always this unpleasant?' I asked tartly.

'No, I'm usually much more unpleasant. Unpleasantness is one of the few pleasures in life left to me.'

'Few pleasures left in life for you? What does that mean, that you're dying?' I'm not normally so blunt but he was getting under my skin.

He didn't answer immediately but stood next to a

well-stocked bar and waved his hand over the array of bottles: scotch, gin, rum, brandy, and vodka, amongst others. 'Help yourself,' he invited.

So, I did. I took a large scotch, single malt Talisker, and added some water and had a drink. Just what I needed on a cold December's night, 'Cheers,' I said but then noticed that he did not have a drink in hand. 'You're not drinking yourself? Is that something to do with what you said, no pleasures left in life?'

'I have been an alcoholic since the age of eighteen. I now have a liver the size of a football,' he said, patting a protuberant belly, 'and my doctor advises me that to drink again will probably kill me.'

'Oh, sorry to hear that,' I answered, but he did not look at all well. He was rheumy eyed and gaunt, with sallow skin hanging from his flesh like badly hung pelmets.

'Are you? I rather doubt it, it was a, what did you call it, a meaningless banality.'

'Good one! So tell me, Uncle, why am I here? Why out of the blue, after years of having nothing to do with me or my dad, do you suddenly invite me to come and stay?'

'Firstly, forget the uncle bit. We are both adults. I am Leonard, you are Richard, and so we shall address each other. Secondly, I shall explain everything, the whys and the wherefores, later. In the meantime, let us at least be civil. Enjoy your drink and then we'll talk after dinner.'

Once again, I meekly did as I was told, although a sense of trepidation was gnawing at my innards like a hungry rat. Already an innate alarm bell was telling me I was making a mistake. You might ask what I was doing there in the first place. Well, it was Christmas and I had nowhere else to go. Bethany, my live-in girlfriend of three years had left me and had gone back to Cardiff. Not that I blame her, apart from that bit about Cardiff, that is. I was homeless. The flat that Bethany and I shared was rented and was way too big and expensive for me to keep on by myself. I say homeless. I was not exactly out on the street but had a room in a B & B which made the cell of a Trappist monk look homely. I was also jobless. A second-hand car business in which I had been a partner had gone belly up with large debts and left me strapped for cash.

So, where to go for Christmas? I would have ended up topping myself if I had to spend it in the B & B, and although my brother Beanie and his wife Alison always invited me 'to come and spend Christmas with us' it was clearly understood that the invitation was never, ever, to be taken up. I'd rather they be honest and simply say, 'We don't like you and don't want you anywhere near us over Christmas.'

Then out of the blue came a card, not a Christmas card, but a plain, white, lined card, with the unsigned handwritten message, 'Come and spend Christmas at Ravensdale House. It will be to your advantage.' It was, I thought, rather peremptory, but I had to look it up in a dictionary just to check if it was the right word. It was. Peremptory, meaning insisting on immediate attention or obedience, especially in a brusquely imperious way. My first thought was to bin it, but the prospect of spending Christmas in the Majestic B & B overrode common sense, so I scribbled OK on the back of the card and posted it back. Consequently, there I was, two days before Christmas having made that fateful journey into the heart of darkness.

In case you are interested, Ravensdale House was

located in the depths of the Edale Valley in the Derbyshire Peak District, some twenty miles from Sheffield where I lived. It was approached by a heavily wooded drive, all but invisible from the road. A mid-nineteenth-century, six-bedroomed, country house, built for a Sheffield factory owner, who declined to spend any money on the exterior so apart from an entrance portico the outside was as plain as a brown paper bag.

I fully expected that the interior would follow suit, hard-faced and intimidating, just like its owner, Uncle Leonard. But, no, I was pleasantly surprised, the décor was light and neutral with plenty of lamps to brighten the darkest corners. The furniture was comfortable, not new, but of a timeless vintage, perfectly suited to the surroundings. The curtains were velvet but in a soft cream, blending into the off-white walls, with bright and colourful oriental carpets laid on polished oak floors.

The dinner that evening, cooked by his housekeeper Mrs Antrim, was good. Medium rare sirloin steak served with boiled new potatoes, asparagus, and peas, although Leonard ate but little.

There was a bottle of Cote de Rhone, velvety smooth, ripe, and supple. I don't know much about wine but what little I did know told me it was a far better wine than ever I could have afforded.

Afterwards, we retired to the parlour and sat in high-backed armchairs either side of a blazing wood fire and played happy families. Leonard handed me a large snifter almost full of Hine brandy, seemingly determined to get my liver to the same state as his in the shortest possible time. Then he opened a cigar box and took a large Cuban cigar, sniffed appreciatively as he rolled it between his figures, snipped the end with a silver cigar cutter, and lit up before offering me the box.

'No, thanks, not for me, they're not good for the health.'

'You think? Winston Churchill smoked ten of these every day, started off the day with a cigar and scotch or brandy with breakfast, drank copious quantities of champagne and brandy, ate excessively, and lived to the ripe old age of ninety-six. Just goes to show that you can't trust a word these doctors tell you.'

'Yet you believe what your doctor has told you about drinking.'

'That is true, but I cannot say that not drinking is doing me any good.'

I took another sip of the excellent brandy. I was feeling the effects of all this drink now but pleasantly so, mellow, and relaxed. 'You said you would tell me what this is all about after dinner. It is now well past dinner.'

'And, so I shall, but like a Charles Dickens novel, I can only tell you by instalments, one chapter at a time.'

'So, go ahead. Chapter One.'

'So, the reason that I have asked you to come and stay here is that I want you to kill me!'

'What? What did you say?'

'You heard me perfectly clearly. Unlike you and your generation, I do not mutter or mumble, I speak with clarity and precision. You heard me perfectly well.'

That pleasant mellow feeling now quickly fled out of the door, my stomach did a lurch, and my heart began to beat fiercely.

'You, you want me to kill you? Like, help you, assisted suicide, is that it?'

'No. I want you, need you, to kill me. To murder me in fact.'

'Mm... murder you, are you mad?'

'I have never been saner. Richard. The deal is this. If you agree to murder me, in which act I shall not assist you in any way, I will name you my heir. This house, the grounds and a not inconsiderable sum of money in banks, stocks, shares and other investments will be yours. You will be a wealthy man, able to live out your life in whatever debauched manner you prefer.'

This was all too much to take in. My mind was a swirling mass of chaos and all I could splutter out was 'But what? Why? I need...' I tailed off lamely. 'Why?'

'The answer to that will be revealed in... further chapters as it were. For now, this is all I can tell you.'

'If, if I refuse, will someone else do it? Beanie?'

'Beanie? You mean Benjamin? Good God, no. He can barely wipe his own backside without that wife of his telling him which hand to use. No, if you do not, death will take its natural course and you will get nothing. Not even an invite to my funeral.'

'I... I don't know what to say. What to think.'

'Of course not, it is a lot take in. Sleep on it and we'll talk again tomorrow. After dinner. Besides, nothing more can be... revealed until after you have met Alice.'

Alice? Who was Alice? A mad wife locked away in the attic. Alice Cooper? Alice in Wonderland?

'Alice?'

'Yes, Alice. Alice is...' a bitter smile without humour crossed his face, 'Alice is our resident ghost.'

It was then that I looked to the door, expecting the nurses to come in and lead him back to his padded cell.

I slept but fitfully that night, the more so after Leonard told me he was 'putting me in Alice's old room' but refused to explain further, except to say that I was the first guest to ever stay at Ravensdale which sounded extremely ominous. Outside the winter winds raged, rattling the windowpanes like skeleton bones, and the old house creaked and groaned like the opening of a coffin lid after years underground.

But no fearsome apparition haunted me that night, nor the following night, in fact it was Christmas Night before Alice came to visit. I awakened in the dark, feeling a presence there in the room with me. I hardly dared turn my head, my heart was pounding fiercely, my stomach roiled and churned, my breathing was shallow and rapid whilst chill fingers of dread insidiously tightened about my heart, the dread oozing like a serpent through the liquid membranes of my soul. The air felt heavy and gelatinous, devoid of oxygen, terror a strangling hangman's knot about my throat.

I am not a churchgoer and it is a long time since I had prayed, but I prayed that night, prayed under my breath. Or at least tried to.

Our Father which art in Heaven,
Hallowed be thy name.
Thy Kingdom come
Thy will be done...
In earth as it is... in ... Heaven...

But I could remember nothing more, except for the one line.

But deliver us from evil

But deliver us from evil!

. . .

Slowly, so slowly, as if of its own volition, my head turned to face the horrors that awaited me.

She stood there, about halfway between my bed and the door. Alice! The resident ghost!

She was a young girl, aged fourteen or fifteen, a girl on the cusp of womanhood, with that prettiness that tells you she would grow up to be a beautiful woman. Except that, apparently, she had never grown up. Alice stood there, tall and slender, hands clasped demurely before her just looking at me as if in curiosity. She wore a yellow, calf-length summer dress with short puff sleeves. Her hair was darkened, as if wet and her skin was pale, almost luminous. She lifted her right hand, wiggled her fingers as if in greeting, smiled a soft smile, and delicately faded away.

It was many minutes before my breathing returned to normal, and I began to wonder if in fact the visitation had been a dream, and, eventually, I managed to persuade myself (delude myself) that yes, it had all been a dream.

But next morning Leonard soon scotched that idea.

'So, you saw her then? Alice?'

'I… I don't know, I might have imagined it.'

'Don't bullshit me, Richard. Give me more credit than that.'

'Yes. Yes, OK, I did see something.'

'Something?' he pressed.

'Alice, I think, yes possibly I saw her. Alice. A young girl?'

'Alice, yes, she's the only ghost we have at the moment, although there is nothing to say that I won't come back and haunt this sad and crumbling pile of stones.'

'OK, so it was Alice. And now you give me chapter two, right?'

'After dinner, as for today we'll go for a walk, the winds have subsided, the sky is clear, and the view from the top of Mam Tor is simply magnificent.'

Well, yes, the view may have been magnificent but all I saw that day was the vision of Alice, whoever she was, indelibly etched in my mind's eye.

As was now customary, after dinner we sat either side of the fire, he somewhat recovered from the exertions of day, it had certainly taken it out of him, he was tired and listless as we got back to the house and he immediately made to his bedroom to lie down.

As usual I had a large brandy, whilst Leonard went through his cigar lighting ritual.

'Don't know much about your family history, do you, Richard?' he said once the cigar was going to his satisfaction.

'Is this chapter two?' I asked.

'You could say that. Or a preface if you will.'

'I know that, many years ago, Granddad and Grandma, your mother and father separated, and the rift was never healed.'

'That is true, what else?'

'That you remained here with Granddad and that Grandma took Joseph, the younger son, my dad, with her when she left.'

'Yes, he always was her favourite. What else?'

'That you and Granddad wanted nothing more to do with… with this side of the family.'

'My father was certainly upset when mother left and was not a man to forgive easily but are you sure the fault was all his? Or mine?'

'How do I know? I wasn't around at the time.'

'All I can say is that the divorce, which was not so easy to come by in those days, was bitter and acrimonious. I don't believe that they ever spoke to each other again. I know for certain that Father did not even attend her funeral.'

'Or vice versa.'

He gave me a look which clearly said, frivolity is not appropriate. Strange, I always thought frivolity to be most appropriate. The alternative is too depressing, like choosing castration over a night indoors with bad television.

'So, two or three years after the divorce, Father married again, to a widow called Emily Proctor, who happened to have a daughter from her previous marriage.'

'Alice!' I exclaimed.

'Yes, exactly. Alice.' He let the word hang in the air, like a vulture circling over a carcass. 'Alice,' he said again, softly but with an underlying menace.

'How old was she then? And you?'

'Oh, I was about nine or ten, she about six or seven.'

'And? Come on, this is like pulling teeth from a donkey.'

'From the outset, Father adored her. Doted on her. She could do no wrong in his eyes, no matter what she did. She was his little angel.'

'And you felt pushed out, right?'

'Wrong! He treated me as he had always done and my new mother, stepmother, could not have been kinder.'

'This is so fucking frustrating. Tell me.'

'Intemperate language will get you nowhere,' he chided, but with a thin smile that told me he enjoyed tormenting me.

'Sorry.'

'I doubt it, the use of profanities is so widespread these days, I fully expect to hear them in the Queen's Speech.'

'Yeah, just get on with it, for Christ's sake.'

'OK. I loathed her. From the day she walked through that front door,' he said, pointing in that direction, 'I detested her, hated her. Could not abide her. There was something about her, something…'

'Evil?'

'Evil? No, quite the opposite, lacking in any sense of personality, insipid, the only way I have been able describe it was that she had a colourless soul.'

'Was she simple then, simple-minded?'

'No, no, she was clever enough. Or cunning enough, to inveigle her way into Father's heart.'

'And you hated her for that?'

'No. I just hated her, it was a visceral loathing, irrespective of anything she did or said.'

'And then she died, she must have done for her… spirit… ghost, whatever, to wander about the place. Even I can work that out.'

'Yes, she died.' As he spoke, burning logs in the fireplace suddenly collapsed with dull crash, sending a shower of sparks spiralling up the chimney and my heart lurched in a sudden jolt.

I did not question him further. I knew we were coming to the climax of his tale and the reasons for his bizarre request that I murder him. He would now tell me in his own time, regardless of whether I pressed him or not. I took a drink. Waiting.

He took a deep draw on the cigar. Examined the inch or so of ash on the end, obviously pondering on the best way to proceed.

'About where your car is parked, there used to be a

pond. Not big, about the size of a swimming pool, perhaps a bit less. One day, a day in August, hot, very hot and humid, Alice was bending over, looking at something in the pond, a fish or frog or maybe nothing at all. I crept up behind her,' my heart began to pound as he spoke, 'and pushed her in. Then I held her head under until she drowned.'

'God, no!'

He appeared not to hear my gasp of horror.

'I waited about half an hour and then ran into the house, shouting 'Alice has fallen in the pond, Alice has fallen in the pond.' I then ran back to the pond, jumped in, it was only about three or four feet deep, and pulled her out.

That way, if my clothes had been wet from the drowning, no one would know. Father was devastated. He took her from my arms and carried her back into the house. A broken man. There was an inquest of course, which concluded she had fainted in the heat and fallen into the pond, Verdict –Accidental death. I was eighteen, she just turned fifteen. Father filled in the pond and then took to drink and so did I.'

'From remorse?'

'Remorse? Good God, no, from happiness. From joy! I could not show it of course, but I felt as though I was floating on air. She was a loathsome child and would have grown up to be a loathsome woman. I did the world a favour.'

The brandy tasted sour in my stomach, and I dropped the glass onto floor, the last dregs spilling out and staining the rug beneath my chair. I'm not often speechless but I was just then. My Uncle Leonard had drowned his stepsister in a pond and then drank to celebrate.

'You think I'm a monster, don't you?'

'Of course I think you're a fucking monster. You murdered your stepsister, drowned her in a pond, what else do you think I could think of you? That you're some kind of a hero?' He just shrugged, unmindful of my opinion. 'So why do you want me to kill you, to ease your conscience?'

'It is a necessary expiation.'

'Expiation?'

'Look it up on your fancy phone. Google it'

I did, expiation – noun, derived from expiate – make amends or reparation (for guilt or wrongdoing).'

'Why not just kill yourself, expiate yourself that way. Why do you need to drag me into it?'

He knocked the ash off his cigar into the ashtray and looked up to the ceiling as if seeking words to explain it to a simpleton. 'As you say, I murdered Alice, it is only by being murdered in turn, can… it be balanced out. A murder for a murder.'

'Tit for tat. An eye for an eye, a tooth for a tooth, is that what you mean?'

'Melodramatically put, but accurately so. It is what Alice wants. Requires!'

'Revenge?'

'No, she feels sorry for me. She knows the only way to expiation is that I be murdered.'

'You have cosy fireside chats about this, do you? You and sister Alice.'

'Believe it as you may. But the offer still stands. Kill me in such a way that I am not an active participant, except to provide a corpse, and I name you my heir. You will be wealthy.'

'But murder, I could go to jail for life. What good is your money then?'

'I'm sure your fertile mind can derive a suitable manner to kill me which will avert suspicion.'

'Not if I make it slow and exceedingly painful which is the way I'm thinking at the moment.'

'Pain for me, as I am, would be meaningless. Just think on this, 'Brightside Motors, your business which so catastrophically failed, will bankrupt you. Your partner Peter Ellis, has cheated you, drawing up the business agreement in such a manner which makes you personally responsible for all debt incurred by the business. A document you foolishly signed without taking legal advice or apparently even reading properly.'

'How, how do you know this?'

'I made it my business to find out. I needed to know what sort of man you are. I needed to know what levers I could pull, what buttons to press. Agree to my proposal and I shall ensure that the bankruptcy goes away.'

'I need time, time to think, it's all too much. I mean, you… killing Alice. Killing you.'

'Of course, think on it. Sleep on it. But do not take too long.'

'How long is too long?'

'Who can say but let us just say that the sands are trickling through the hourglass ever more swiftly.'

Well, I certainly couldn't sleep on it, but I thought about it all right. I could hardly think about anything else, not with everything swirling around my brain in a maelstrom.

To wit: My Uncle Leonard is a cold-blooded murderer; he killed Alice, his fifteen-year-old stepsister, who legally if not genetically is my Aunt; afterwards he drank to celebrate the fact; Aunt Alice is now a ghost, apparently telling him to get himself murdered in order to expiate his crime; and he wants me to murder him, in order to achieve said expiation.

Why should I risk my liberty, and possibly sanity, by accommodating this bizarre request?

There seems to be a lot of money involved.

My own money situation is beyond desperate, but how can I kill Leonard?

More importantly, how can I kill Leonard and get away with it?

They say that the truth is like poetry, but such poetic truth I can well do without. On top of all that, Alice came visiting again. I lay there, eyes closed but not sleeping and felt her presence but without the terrors of the night before, somehow calm and serene. She stood closer to me this time, about four feet away, smiling gently at me, such a pretty smile and held out her hand as if to touch me.

Taking a deep breath, in turn I held out my own hand. Tentatively, timidly she placed her hand in mine. How do you describe what it feels like to hold hands with a ghost? Ethereal? That's correct but hardly informative. It was like a soft breath across my palm, neither cold nor warm, the slightest of sensations, enough to say our hands were touching but no more. I gently closed my hand about hers, but it was like trying to hold smoke. She smiled again, took her hand away, held them together before her chest as though pleading and, as before, delicately faded, a wisp of smoke wafted away by a gentle summer breeze.

As much as possible I avoided Leonard for the next two days, walking around the wooded grounds and gardens, or, as on the second day, walking down to the village for a pint at the 'Cheshire Cheese'. The locals looked at me curiously but did not speak other than a grunted hello in response to mine, although the landlord did ask if I had walked or driven from Ravensdale House. Without being told, everyone in the village seemed to know I was a guest up there.

Every night now, Alice came to visit, she sat on the end of the bed, making not a dent in the covers but there was an insubstantial, minute sense of weight, of a presence sitting there. On another night she woke me by stroking my cheek, a feather-light touch and it began to dawn on me that Alice was becoming attracted to me.

But what to do about Leonard, I had more or less decided to follow out his wishes and kill him. But how? The obvious usual suspects: stabbing, the lead pipe in the library, shooting, poison, all were simply that –obvious to even the most dim-witted plod. There was (a pity) no pond to push him in, that would have been poetic justice and we did not go on walks across the many gritstone outcrops dotting the area so I could push him over the edge.

On the third day I told him 'OK. I'll do it,' as much for Alice's sake as his. And mine, money is a powerful incentive when bankruptcy looms and your entire worldly possessions can fit into two suitcases and some cardboard boxes stashed in the boot of the Saab.

'Excellent,' was all he said and made straight for the study, presumably to write his will. The next day he seemed much frailer and asked me to drive him into the town of Bakewell, a thirty-minute drive away, to deposit the will with his solicitors. We took the Rolls as he refused to go in the Saab.

'It looks like a toy pram. I'm not going to be seen out in that.'

I have to say I did enjoy driving the Rolls, although I did feel somewhat like a chauffeur, what with Leonard lording it up in the back seat.

I suppose I should have asked to read the will, just to make sure he was telling me the truth because for all I knew he might have been a bankrupt himself, or the will might say that in the event of his sudden unexplained death, the police should look no further than me. I have always been a trusting soul, much good it does, look at the mess that good friend Peter left me in.

When we got back to the house, he got out and walked round the front of the car, I was sorely tempted to put my foot down and run over him but decided against it, didn't want to damage the beautiful paintwork.

This is probably a good time to mention the entrance hall and staircase, which are very germane to the rest this story. The hall was much larger than the exterior might suggest, almost fifteen metres wide and ten deep with the ground floor rooms being high, five or six or metres, it made for a very impressive space, a statement of power and money, without actually costing that much, A wide staircase led up to a gallery around three sides of the hall, about which were placed the bedrooms. Leonard's room was to the right of the staircase, my room, Alice's room, was next door, but nearer to the stairs.

It was the morning of New Year's Eve when I pushed Leonard down those grandiose stairs. It was totally unplanned. I came out of my room as the same time as he and saw him at the head of the stairs, wavering as if trying to gain his balance before descending. Without thinking I ran up behind him and shoulder charged him in the back. He flew down the stairs, tumbling and twisting, then he crashed into the wall of the half landing and carried on down the next flight where he lay still and unmoving. I ran after him, exultant, I had done it.

But as I reached him, he groaned and opened one eye.

'Nice try, Richard, close but no cigar,' he gasped. 'Now phone an ambulance, I think I've broken my arm.'

As it turned out his arm was not broken but more to the point, neither was his neck. What to do, what to do? That night, Alice came and lay beside me on the bed. We did not touch but we lay face to face as she smiled into my eyes. As crazy as it sounds, Alice, a ghost, was falling in love with me, you might say it was a just a teenage crush on possibly the only man who had ever come into her life (death?) but I do believe it was much deeper than that.

It was now obvious that Leonard was a very sick man, so I needed to get a move on as if he died on me before I could kill him, all could come to nought. I mean, although the will naming me as his heir was deposited with his solicitors, there was nothing to stop him retracting it on his deathbed while dying from natural causes if he thought I was not keeping to my side of the contract.

At last, an idea came to me. It was like this: one morning I was rummaging around the former stables, now garage-cum-storeroom and opened up an old tin trunk. Inside were some climbing boots, long since grown mouldy and mildewed, an anorak, rusting carabineers, and other climbing hardware and three coils of climbing ropes. Rope! That was it, hang the old bastard, just as they hanged murderers in the good old days. From a grey rope intertwined with red thread, slightly less than a half-inch thick, I cut off about twelve feet, tied a bowline to one end (as a climber, a knot he would know), and passed a loop of rope through the eye of the bowline to form a noose and took it up to my room.

I was flexing the rope between my fingers to loosen it up when Alice glided in. No other word so perfectly describes how Alice moved. Glided! She saw the rope, guessed my intentions, and gave me a vibrant smile, nodding her head in agreement. So, everything was in place. All I needed was the opportunity. By the way, it's a complete myth that ghosts only come out at night, I mean, why shouldn't they come out during the day? They're not vampires are they? The only thing is, they are harder to see in the daylight!

Fortune favours the brave. It also favours the vigilant. I began to monitor Leonard's schedule, searching for that opportune moment and it did not take long. It had become his habit to take a nap in his bedroom after lunch, usually soup or sandwiches prepared by Mrs Antrim before she went home for the afternoon, coming back about four. After an hour or so, he would emerge, still a bit sleepy and groggy from his medication. He had to pass my room – Alice's room – to get to the stairs.

I waited for him, heard his bedroom door open, and as he passed by me, I quickly dropped the noose about his neck, tightened it and reaching between his thighs upended him over the banisters and into the stairwell, bracing myself against the banisters, the rope wrapped around my hand and arm to stop his fall. A jerk and the rope quivered like a live thing for a second or two. I then tied the rope to the handrail, and it was done. Dear Uncle Leonard had gone to wherever child killers go. I hope it was somewhere very, very hot.

I quickly ran down to the Saab and drove into the village. In the village shop I bought a loaf of granary bread, milk, a jar of coffee and the 'Daily Mail,' the paper that Leonard read. I pass no comment on that fact. On the way back I stopped at the 'Cheshire Cheese' for a pint without being too obvious about it, I was making sure that I was seen in the village and the pub at the presumed time of Leonard's death.

Once back at the house, I saw that Leonard was still hanging around, so I rang the police and ambulance,

'I've just come back from the village and found my uncle hanging from the stairs, I think he must have killed himself.'

I was, of course, interviewed by the police. Why was I staying at the house they asked, and I explained that Uncle Leonard had wanted to heal a long-standing family rift before he died. No, he had never mentioned killing himself, but it was obvious that he was a very ill man, in continuous pain, so it would be understandable if he felt like killing himself, but even so, it was a tremendous shock to find him hanging there in the hallway. No, I had not seen a copy of his will, and I had no idea what it contained, which was true enough.

It soon became clear that the police had no other thoughts beyond the supposition that Leonard had in fact taken his own life.

At the subsequent inquest, his doctor, Dr Mallory told the coroner that Leonard had terminal cancer of the liver, which had metastasized to his gall bladder and colon, he was diabetic and had been treated for depression and was in constant pain, necessitating massive dosages of morphine, the obvious inference being that he had taken his own life.

Alice actually helped to substantiate that opinion, when she saw me with the rope, she led me down to Leonard's study and pointed to an old book on the shelf. It was entitled 'A Handbook of Hanging', published in 1928 and written by somebody called Charles Duff. It was exactly as it said in the title, 'being a short introduction to the fine art of Execution and containing much useful information on Neck-breaking, Throttling, Strangling, Asphyxiation, Decapitation, and Electrocution: as well as Data and Wrinkles for Hangmen. The author further enjoined 'ALL VERY PROPER TO BE READ AND KEPT IN EVERY FAMILY' and 'Dislocation of the Neck is the ideal to be aimed at.'

Charming! But the book did enable me to accurately gauge the length of 'drop' to give him, guessing he weighed about ten stone, so a six-foot drop would ensure the 'ideal' dislocation of the neck.

So, before the police arrived, I went into Leonard's bedroom and placed the book, open on the 'drop table' page, by his bedside drawer for them to find.

The Coroner's verdict? Suicide.

Shortly afterwards I received a letter from Day and Darkes-Hyde, Leonard's solicitors in Bakewell, inviting me to make an appointment to discuss the Last Will and Testament of one Leonard Gatehouse. After the usual specious banalities, sorry to hear about your Uncle blah, blah, blah, I proved my identity by means of my passport and we got down to business.

'Your Uncle's will, Mr Gatehouse,' Elizabeth Darkes-Hyde said,' names you as…' a deadly pause and for a heart-stopping moment I thought she was going to say, 'names you as his killer,', 'as his principal beneficiary. There are some minor bequests to Cancer Research and the Edale Mountain Rescue Team but apart from those bequests, the balance of the estate comes to you, including Ravensdale House, which is clear of all mortgage or other financial encumbrances.

'Good. How soon can I sell it, can you arrange that? Or recommend somebody who can?'

'Sell? Oh no, Mr Gatehouse, the will is quite explicit, there is a restrictive covenant, and the property must remain within the Gatehouse family? Do you have children, Mr Gatehouse?'

'Me? No, leastwise not that I know of, but you never know.'

She gave me one of those looks, a 'flippancy is not appropriate' look. 'In the event of your decease without issue, the property will devolve to your nearest relative, be it a sibling or the apparent next of kin, in perpetuity.'

Why can't these people speak English, why not say, If I die without having sired children, the house will go to Beanie or in the event he has carked it as well, to his sprogs, or to their kids and so on ad infinitum for ever and ever, amen.

'You may live in the property or lease it out, as you wish, but Ravensdale House can never be sold.'

'Mmmm, bummer.'

Elizabeth Darkes-Hyde then passed over a Statement of Account, detailing the actual cash and other financial assets of the estate, and of course, details of legal fees and solicitors' costs to be deducted from the estate. Judging by the size of the solicitor's costs, I was clearly in the wrong business and was reminded of a true Yorkshireman's battle cry, an indignant 'How much?'

Also, Leonard had lied about the value of his estate,

although a considerable sum, it was nowhere near enough to make me the promised 'wealthy man,' able to live out my life in whatever debauched manner I preferred. He had however, dealt with the bankruptcy threat.

I still had to find a means of income, so I leased Ravensdale House to an outdoor pursuits company, you know, they take clients out rock climbing, hill walking, caving, canoeing, activities like that. It seemed to be successful. The rents came every month without fail, so I have no complaints there.

As for myself, there was enough capital to start a property renovation business in Sheffield. I bought old properties, usually at auction, and renovated them, putting in new electrics, kitchens, and bathrooms, decorating, tidying up the garden, that sort of thing. I didn't do much of the work myself but acted as project manager and after some trial and error, put together a reliable team of self-employed tradesmen. It went well, giving me a steady profit and I bought a three bedroom cottage overlooking the Mayfield Valley, on the outskirts of the city. There was a nice patio where I could sit and watch the sunset go down with a glass of fine red wine in hand, often a Cote de Rhone, one thing I did bring from Ravensdale House was Leonard's rather fine wine collection which won't last forever but enables me to explore and discover what I really like.

I kept the Rolls, a bit ostentatious I know, but I enjoyed driving it around. I kept the Saab too, It is pleasant to drive around the Peak District countryside in summer with the hood down.

The only drawback to my idyllic life is that I am unable to sustain a relationship, girlfriends never feel comfortable in the house, complaining of an 'atmosphere'. I can't even keep a cat or dog there.

You see, about three months after I moved into the cottage, I awoke to spectral clawing at my face. Alice stood there, how she had found me, or how she got here (ghost train?) I can't say but she obviously believed that I had abandoned her at Ravensdale House, and she was angry, very, very, angry.

For as the poet Congreve says:
Heav'n has no rage like love to hatred turned,
Nor Hell a fury like a woman scorned.

And she is definitely, most definitely, here to stay, seemingly determined to make my life as miserable as possible.

THAT SUMMER, 1941

It was one of those brilliant summers of youth, the summer of 1941, when every day was full of bright sunshine, the skies were eternally blue, and the horizons of a ten-year-old boy's imagination knew no bounds.

At the end of the previous year, I had been evacuated from London, along with my sister Chrissie, to Upper Marchlow, a village in the countryside somewhere near Gloucester. I never did get the geography exactly right.

We were billeted with a formidable old lady we had to call Auntie May. She lived in a large rambling house, dark and gloomy which smelled musty and dank, of dead things rotting in the wainscot. Auntie May herself was kindly enough, but she was a childless widow from a different generation with no idea how to deal with boisterous children released from the grey, bombed streets and dangerous skies of the East End. But she did try, bless her, whatever else, Auntie May did try her best. She and Mrs Pickles, the elderly cook. I only wish I had appreciated it more. But all that is past, too late to make amends.

From the back of the ivy-covered house, Auntie May's garden ran a great distance down to the woods. Close to the house it was arrayed in formal terraces, with clipped hedges, lawns that once had been billiard table smooth, and a small statue of a water nymph pouring water from a jug.

Further down the garden changed, from the formal to the informal: a walled herb garden, curving beds full of flowers I that had never seen outside of a flower sellers barrow, lilacs, lupins, dahlias, plump headed chrysanthemums, borders heavy with the scent of purpling lavender, a small orchard bursting with a promise of bountiful apples and pears and thick with yellow-jacketed wasps, the summer days full of sunshine, birdsong, and the industrious buzz of bees and brightly coloured butterflies flittering back and forth from bloom to bloom.

Even though most of the garden had been given over to vegetables, there were still lots of flowers. That is what I remember the most, the flowers and the bright bursting yellows and reds and violets of those summer blossoms.

The garden must once have been immaculate, but now that two of Auntie May's gardeners had been called up, there were signs that Ancient Williams, the one remaining gardener, was finding the upkeep too hard for just one man: weeds appeared where none had ever dared before, the joints between the paviours were filling with moss, and the lawns were pockmarked with mole hills and strewn with white-faced daisies.

At the bottom of the garden was a small summer house set in a lower lawn and the garden then just petered out by a thick yew hedge with an arched gateway that led into the intense dark wood of beech and oak trees. I loved that dark secret coppice, with its hint of danger, of unseen things lurking in the undergrowth, a playground for my wild exuberances.

To a city boy who had only ever seen trees in a tiny public park, the wood was an adventure, filled with leaf-carpeted hollows, sinister shadows, deep silence and a treasure-land of birds and endless trees to climb. Deep in the depths of the wood there was a secret and haunted place, where the sun could not penetrate, and the chill of the shadowy moss-clad black tree trunks was a place of dark imaginings. Deep in the wood, there was a deep, round pond, black peaty water, green scum flecked, always hidden in the deepest of deep shade, a place of trolls and hag-faced witches. The trees overhung the pond from all sides, gnarled roots clawing into the black waters like troll fingers hunting for fish and small reptiles – or small boys – to seize and devour. The banks of the pond were steep and slickly muddy, leaf strewn and treacherous underfoot.

It was by the summer house that I first saw the little girl. I had never seen her before. I thought I knew all the children from the village by now, but this one I had never seen. She stood stock still, staring at me as I chased a bumble bee from flower to flower.

She was small and pale, with long flowing yellow-gold hair the colour of the ripened corn in the fields beyond the woods. Her dress was pale pink in colour, full and flouncy, mid-calf in length, tied with a large bow about her waist. She held her hands before her, staring unblinkingly at me as I approached her. I judged her to be about my age or maybe a little younger.

I was about fifty feet from her when her eyes suddenly widened and she turned on her heels and ran away, skipping lightly across the dappled grass through the archway and into the wood.

'Wait' I called after her. 'Wait on.' I ran after her, intrigued. I was bored that day and any diversion was welcome. I ran through the archway, wondering which path she might have taken, but even though I was only seconds behind her there was no sign of her.

The sunlight rippled darkly through the heavy overcroft of branches and thick foliage, the temperature dropping suddenly in the murkled shade. The left-hand path led arrow-straight through the wood and out onto Marchlow Lane, a half mile or so above the village. If the girl had taken that path, I would be able to see her clear all the way to the lane. The right hand trail led around in a curve tight against the hedge and wall of Auntie May's property before exiting over a stile into Farmer Hogarth's upper fields.

Another path ran almost central to the archway, deep into the gloom of the darkwoods and the troll hole. This path was little used, thick undergrowth snagged across the winding path and anyone running through that path would have made considerable noise.

I stopped to listen… wood pigeons cooed from the canopy above, I could hear the high-pitched drone of a Spitfire taking off from the airbase over at Tideburn Magna and an asthmatic tractor slowly wheezed its way around Hogarth's fields but no sight or sounds of a fleeing girl.

'Hello,' I called, but my voice echoed hollowly back from the shadow-blackened copse. I ran down the right-hand path looking to both sides, thinking that she might be hiding although her pink dress would be hard to conceal, even in the thickest of bushes or coppicewood. I ran all the way to Hogarth's fields. Beyond the stile a right of way ran across the fields and the mysterious little girl would be exposed out in the open fields if she had gone that way. But there was no sight of her.

Cursing the curses of ten-year-old boys, I ran back again, brambles whipping at my bare legs raising welts and scratches as though I had been savaged by sharp clawed beast. Quite why I was expending so much energy on such a trivial matter I cannot say. I ran all the way as far as Marchlow Lane, without catching so much as a glimpse of her.

Annoyed with myself, I trudged back, kicking at stones and twigs. A large magpie sitting on a branch cawed derisively at me; I threw a stone at it, missing by some margin even though I thought my aim was true. A village boy had told me it was immense bad luck to kill a magpie, but I didn't care.

It was two days before I saw the little girl again. This time I was actually in the summer house trying to read one of the books that Auntie May had given me: 'Ivanhoe' by Sir Walter Scott. My reading wasn't very good at school and Auntie May was trying to help me, I would read a passage or a chapter a day and after dinner, we would talk about what I had read, and she would explain the big words for me.

From the corner of my eye, I saw her peer through the yew-hedge archway before making a nervous step or two into the garden. She didn't see me at first, hidden as I was in the shadow of the summer house. She wore the same pink dress, her hair this time ties up in bunches with red ribbon. Carefully I put the book down and slid out of the summer house and around the back.

The girl was twenty feet or so into the garden when I quietly stepped out from behind the summer house.

'Wotcha,' I called out, ''Hello.'

She started as though shot, hesitated a second or two, and then turned and fled back through the arch. I ran after her, but my bootlace had become untied, my heel slipped loose in the shoe, and I stumbled over onto my knees. By the time I got to the archway she had vanished again.

I ran a short way down all the pathways, still intrigued as to how she could vanish so completely, but again there was no sign of her.

The next time I saw her was three days later. I was in the wood itself, deep inside the darkest reaches, close by the troll hole and the other haunted realms.

I had climbed a tree, imagining myself captain of a pirate ship when I saw her coming down the pathway from Marchlow Lane, wearing a different dress this time, cornflower blue in colour but still the same flouncy bouncy style. I slid down the tree and slowly crept along the path, crouching Red Indian style like the Apache warriors in the cowboy films I had seen at the Saturday morning cinema matinee.

I reached the end of the path by the archway, but she was nowhere to be seen, not in Auntie May's garden by the summer house, nor along either of the pathways, left and right. Nowhere.

This time I wasn't going to play her games and set off back down the path towards the troll hole. Slowly I skirted the pond, senses sharp and alert, ready to flee if the troll emerged from the darkening deep waters.

Suddenly, there she was, half hidden in the shadow of an oak, staring at me again.

'Hello,' I said softly, careful not to startle her.

'I know you,' she said nervously, her voice barely

carrying, 'I know you, you're that evacuee boy from London.'

'Yeah, so what.'

'You're the one as drowned in this pond. I've never ever seen a ghost before.'

FROM DARKNESS AND HORROR COMES LIGHT

The only time my father ever spoke to me about his time as a prisoner in the notorious Nazi death camp of Auschwitz was the day of my sister Susan's wedding. He had had a glass or two or three of champagne and was feeling mellow and content over his only daughter's happiness.

He hardly ever drank, my father, he once said that after all the horrors he had seen at Auschwitz, if ever he started drinking, he would never stop. But that day, after champagne, for the once and only time, he talked about the horrors of the death camp.

I should say that this happened more than thirty years ago and that my father has been dead these fifteen years or more. But what he told me, all those years ago, has lingered in my consciousness like an ever-present dream or I should say nightmare; that such horrors could be inflicted by humans on fellow human beings is beyond imagining.

Of course, I have read about the holocaust, seen films such as 'Schindler's List' and watched documentaries on the Discovery Channel, but the raw impact of my father's own experience far outweighs anything to be read or seen on the television. And of all the dreadful vile, inhuman things of which he spoke one incident, in its way insignificant when compared to the mass murder of six million people, stood out and has lived with me ever since. As, I'm sure, it haunted him.

We were sitting out in the garden. It was early summer evening, the day of my sister Sue's wedding. My mother was dozing in her chair by the window, Sue and her husband Gerald had gone off on honeymoon to Scotland, (no honeymoons in St Lucia or other exotic locations in those days). My father had drunk his champagne and was in a relaxed, contemplative mood.

The evening sun slanted through the whispering leaves of the elm trees at the bottom of the garden and the birds were carolling their evensong before settling down. The evening was so quiet and peaceful, no traffic noise, only the vibrant song of the birds and brilliant orange sun-setting-streaks splashed across the clear azure sky.

My father tilted his head to listen to the birds: a pair of doves cooed to each other, and a phalanx of sparrows and thrushes warbled away in the sunset-stroked elms.

'You know,' he said quietly, as if not to disturb the birds in their exuberance, drawing deeply on his celebratory wedding day cigar, 'they say that birds never sing at Auschwitz.'

I felt a thrill like high-powered electricity running through me. 'You were there? In Auschwitz?'

I knew he had been, my mother once told me and warned me never to ask him about it. 'Too painful,' she said.

'Aye. Aye, I was there.' He repeated it, three or four more times. 'Aye, I was there.'

I said nothing, afraid to break his mood.

'I never thought then that I'd get to see this,' he waved his cigar about airily, leaving a con trail of blue smoke. 'I mean, family, house, daughter happily married, all that.'

He had been in the RAF, he said, the navigator in a Liberator bomber, flying out of Brindisi in northern Italy on bombing missions over German positions in Warsaw during the Polish Uprising in June 1944.

'We dropped our bombs OK, turned back for home then we were caught in a searchlight cone and hit by anti-aircraft fire. The skipper, Frank Manning, he was killed outright. Billy Maple, co-pilot, lovely lad only twenty-two, he didn't make it out. Kenny the Aussie engineer, I saw him jump but never saw a parachute open. I bailed out and watched the ship dive into the ground like a blazing torch.' He stopped for a minute or two, lost in his memories, seeing again in his mind's eye his blazing aircraft and his crew of mates in their final dying moments.

The sun sank lower and as dusk crept in, the birds fell silent. He reached down from his chair and rubbed at his right ankle, something I had seen him do many times before, sitting in his armchair, watching television, reaching down, almost sub-consciously, to rub and massage his ankle but never bore it any mind.

'I landed in a field, landed heavily, went over on my ankle, still not sure to this day whether I broke it or not. Still gives me gyp even now when rain is forecast. Anyway, I crawled away from my 'chute and found shelter in a barn. The next day the farmer found me, fed me, hid me behind a high bale of hay when the Germans came looking. Brave man he was. The Jerries would have shot him and all his family if they'd found me. Never knew his name. Never asked.'

He sighed, and I sensed that now he had started talking, he would never cease until it was all out after being bottled up inside him all those years and now unstoppably flowing free like lava from an erupting volcano.

'After four days, a Polish resistance group, three men and a woman, came for me. The farmer must have contacted them somehow. They half carried me as I limped along, still in agony from my ankle. We moved by night, from farm to farm, sometimes through thick forests and woods, heading to the east, the intention to get behind the Russian front line so that they could repatriate me; they were supposed to be our allies back then, the Russians. Then I think we were betrayed because a German patrol found us hidden in yet another barn and took no retribution on the farmer for hiding us. They beat us up pretty bad. I was in borrowed clothes but still had my dog-tags on, you know identity tags,' he said, rubbing at his shirt where the dog-tags would have laid against his chest. 'The resistance guys, they beat up them badly, raped the woman, and then shot them all. Left her lying naked in the mud. Me, they didn't know what to do with, so they handed me over to the Gestapo in case I was a spy or secret agent.

'The Gestapo, they were not gentle, wanting me to tell them what I knew about the resistance. But I knew nothing of course, apart from the guys who rescued me, and they were now dead.' And for the first time I realized the significance of my father's damaged hand, he had no nails on three fingers of his left hand. All these years I thought it was because of an accident or at worst a war wound. Which I suppose it was.

'No,' he repeated, 'they were not gentle at all,' he

said, rubbing at his ankle again, and I suspect that the Gestapo tortured his injured ankle as well.

He was moved from one camp to another until finally he was transported to Auschwitz.

'Why Auschwitz? I thought Auschwitz, was, you know, for Jews, I mean we aren't Jews?'

'Oh no, it was mainly Jews of course but they had others there, a British Naval officer for one, how the Royal Navy got to be in a death camp in the middle of Poland, I don't know but there he was. Gypsies, Russian prisoners of war, they were treated just as badly as the Jews, criminals, mental defectives, all sorts.'

Twilight had set in and a pair of swifts darted by, hunting the last of the day's insects. An early bright moon glowed crystal silver in the darkening sky.

'People say Auschwitz must have been Hell on earth, but that is just words. Words! There are no words. Or not enough words. Auschwitz was just that. Auschwitz!

My father (I could never think of him as Dad in this context) spoke on about Auschwitz, the transport trains, cattle trucks packed solid with deportees from all over Nazi occupied Europe, two, four, or five days in transit without food, water, or sanitary facilities. Emaciated, starved skeletons driven from the ghettos, driven onto the trucks with kicks and threats or sometimes deceit, to be met at Auschwitz by SS guards and snarling Alsatian dogs trained to attack, driven with whips and rifle butts into line for selection, to the right meant immediate death in the gas chambers, to the left meant temporary reprieve as slave labour, twins to be sent to the medical block for Dr Josef Mengele, the Angel of Death, to perform his obscene experimentations, the relentless gas chambers and the four crematoriums belching out their evil choking black smoke twenty-four hours a day.

'I was put to work in the 'reception' area where those chosen for death were made to undress before gassing, told that they were to take a shower before being put to work. I had to sort out the clothes, pile the shoes in one heap, coats in another, underwear, spectacles, all would be sorted, cleaned, and sent to Germany for distribution to the German people. Women were put to work carefully unstitching the yellow Star of David from the sleeves of jackets and coats. Sometimes I had to sort out the contents of the suitcase the deportees had brought with them in the mistaken belief that they were being 're-settled'. The women had their heads shaved and the hair made into quilts for U-boats crews and then they were herded into the gas chambers.'

He spoke without passion, as though all anger and outrage had been drained away by the enormity of his experiences. Cold precision, dead emotions. It was now completely dark. Venus shone diamond-bright to the west, a high moon rising with Jupiter in attendance.

'Even then, facing death, the women suffered yet more indignity, the guards assaulting them… sexually, searching for hidden valuables in their… you know… privates.' His cigar had gone out unnoticed some time before, and he used the excuse of relighting it to cover his embarrassment at such an unpleasantly intimate detail.

'There was one of the SS gas chamber detail, a Captain, SS Hauptstürmfűhrer Üwe Hassler, a tall cold-eyed blond Nazi thug. Cold eyes as dead as a fish left too long on the fishmonger's slab, detached, devoid of feeling, humanity, compassion, devoid of life even. He didn't indulge in the sexual humiliation of the women, I suppose because it was as if he was already dead himself, indifferent, dead within, already grave-cold, grave-dead. How do you even begin to describe such a creature, beyond all human feeling or emotion?'

An owl hooted in the copse at the end of the road, followed by a shriek as the owl took a vole or young rabbit, as if to answer, a harbinger of death and evil.

'And then, one day, sometime early in the year 1945, the most extraordinary thing. Hassler came alive. One moment, he stood there, cold, unemotional, barely even seeing those whom he was sending to their deaths. The next, struck by lightning! His cold dead eyes burst alight. All the scales of unfeeling, of deathly uncaring numbness, fell away, it was like he had been encased in clay, a clay mould, transparent, and suddenly the mould broke away and sunlight burst out from him. Fanciful descriptions, I know, but that's exactly how it was. I was no more than ten feet away from him when it happened. Hassler had fallen in love, love at first sight. You read about that, love at first sight, and you dismiss it as romantic nonsense, Mills and Boon stuff, I mean, your mother hated the sight of me at first, not so sure she still doesn't sometimes,' he laughed with a soft smile, 'but Hauptstürmführer Hassler, he fell so deep, he was a different man.

'I never knew her name, not even sure that Hassler did, certainly not then he didn't. She was a Jewess. I heard later that she was Dutch, from Rotterdam, one of the last of the Dutch Jews to be rounded up and sent to the gas chambers. She wasn't in any way beautiful, but then, I don't suppose any woman is after years of starvation and fear and days incarcerated in a cattle truck without the most basic of sanitary facilities, not even a bucket.

Like all the other women she was slowly undressing, shy and fearful, frightened by the taunts of the SS and their Lithuanian counterparts, it was not only the German who hated and persecuted the Jews you know: Poles, Ukrainians, Lithuanians, from every country they invaded the Nazis always found willing accomplices to murder and brutalise the Jews. Anyway, this girl, for that's all she was, no more than twenty or twenty-one certainly, she was of medium height, skin and bones mostly, blonde hair not yet shaved. She was undressing when Hassler noticed her. As I say, everything fell away from him, his eyes just burst alight and he called her over to him. 'Du, hier komst,' he said, pointing to her. Fearful she walked over, trying to cover herself. Hassler said nothing more, just pointed to her clothes, ordered her to dress again and led her away, much to the amazement of the guards, but he outranked them and there was nothing they could do. He just led her out, saved her from the jaws of death for want of a better way of putting it.

Where he took her, I don't know, not to his quarters in the SS barracks, I'm sure, but there were plenty of stores and other places. They became lovers of course, although whether she loved him who can say, but he saved her life so perhaps she did.'

'Hassler moved her about the camp, putting her to work in different areas so she would not be noticed, in the Canada barracks for instance where all the sorted clothes were sent, but inevitably, about six or seven weeks later they were found out, betrayed no doubt for an extra slice of bread by an inmate or an SS fanatic concerned about racial purity of the Master Race. Relations with a Jewess, sexual relations, was punishable by death. All the camp were ordered to witness the executions, lined up in shivering ranks about the gallows in the main square. They killed her first, hanging her by her feet from the gallows whilst they beat her with clubs, breaking her bones before finally forcing sand and dirt into her mouth and nose and choking her as all the while Hassler had to watch, tears of anguish streaming down his face. Then they hanged him alongside her, still in his black SS uniform but with all the insignia ripped off. They hanged him slow, no drop, twisting and squirming at the end of the rope. Took him a long time to die. They left them hanging there for three days as a warning to everyone.

'I cannot say I felt pity for him, after all, he had led so many to their deaths, but for once, in all the horror and death and murder, for a few brief weeks, there was a spark of light, of humanity, amongst all that death there was life.

'Of all I saw at Auschwitz, all the horrors and killings, the murder of that spark, that love, perverted as it might have been, struck me most of all. Love is all and the Nazis even murdered that.'

He fell silent, exhausted, and drained. I got up, walked over to my Dad and gave him the biggest hug I could.

Love is all.

INCIDENT AT GRETNA GREEN

It happened a long time ago, more than forty years ago in fact. I am now seventy-eight years old and have not got long to go as the cancer takes a tighter grip, but from that day to this, I have never told a living soul, not even my own dear wife. So now is perhaps the right time to relate what happened that May morning all those years ago, memories of which are as clear in my mind as they were the day it happened.

I had been to a series of meetings in Edinburgh and had then to travel across country to Carlisle to attend a conference there before going back to London. I took the early morning milk train and settled down in my corner seat by the window so I could watch the passing countryside, never having been to Scotland before. However, I was so tired after two days of intense meetings, and the previous evening's dinner with the client had gone on much later than I had wished and with rather more wine than I am used to, and so it was not long before the rhythmic swaying of the train lulled me to sleep.

The slamming of train doors and the tramp of many boots woke me up and the carriage door opened and four soldiers, with full kitbags came in without acknowledging us. I say us because at some time during the journey a little old lady had boarded the train and was sitting in the window seat opposite me.

The soldiers put their kitbags up on the luggage rack and settled down, chattering away amongst themselves, their Scots accents so thick I could barely understand a word. The little old lady watched them intently. She was small and birdlike, her eyes following the soldiers one by one as they spoke, but never saying a word herself.

The soldiers were smart, their uniforms new, but somehow outdated, anachronistic, they wore ill-fitting thick khaki tunics, puttees wrapped around their calves and caps with a checkerboard band around the brim and a ribbon of tartan down at the back. From the cap badges I could see that they were from the Royal Scots Regiment and their enthusiasm and pride in their regiment shone out like a beacon of hope.

The soldiers, some of them no more than boys, smoked incessantly, which annoyed me because I was sure I had taken a No Smoking carriage but there were no signs on the window so there was nothing I could say.

I could hear the shouts and chatter and the clump of boots from more soldiers in the adjoining carriages and my nice peaceful idyll across the Scottish countryside was shattered, so I closed my eyes again and dozed off.

Then I heard a strident, fear-tinged shout, 'We're running into another train!'

The words had hardly registered before there was a terrible crash, all the windows of the carriage imploded, and the carriage leapt into the air, all of us hurled across the carriage and onto the floor. The flying glass had caused some cuts. One young lad had blood streaming down his face from a nasty head cut and another had a cut hand but the rest of us seemed alright. We were winded and shocked of course, then the carriage rolled over and tumbled down an embankment. The carriage was now on its side, so we clambered up and out through the window. I had to help the old lady who although of course deeply shocked was unhurt as was I apart from a bruise or two and some abrasions. Still she said not a word.

The wreckage from the crash was piled up high and it looked as though the leading carriages from both trains had been telescoped into a twisted, buckled mass of wood and steel, crushed together into an unrecognisable scrapheap some thirty feet high.

The cries and screams of the injured and dying echoed along the wreckage as terror-stricken men, dazed and confused, broken-boned and bleeding staggered along the trackside. Bodies had been thrown clear of the wreck. There was one body, a young lad, clearly dead from a broken neck, another so mangled it was hard to tell it had been a human being. Many were still trapped in the wreckage, especially those further to the front of the train. Their cries for help, their cries of pain and anguish live with me still. The uninjured scrambled along the wrecked coaches, trying to free their friends trapped inside, hammering helplessly at doors too buckled to ever open again, through windows crushed to mere slots a few inches wide.

Others wandered about, dazed and confused. Another young lad, he looked no more than sixteen years, sat at the trackside, head in hands, crying uncontrollably. Officers rushed up and down trying to bring some order to the chaos but without great success, there was simply too much damage, too much distress, too many injuries, too many deaths.

The impact of the crash had pushed sections of the two trains across the tracks of the northbound carriageway. And then above the screams and cries and screech of tortured metal came the onrushing roar as another train bore down upon the wreckage and carriages strewn across its track. The Glasgow Express ploughed into the wrecked trains at full speed, smashing the wreckage aside, hurling it back into the mass of dazed men by the trackside, a piece of flying metal hit a soldier standing next to me and decapitated him instantly. A whole carriage smashed back, crushing countless men, taking with it all the men who had been in my carriage.

Never in my life have I felt so helpless, so distraught to see those fine, laughing young men taken away in an instant, crushed to a pulp. Another body lay spreadeagled as though crucified across the top of the wrecked carriage, unmarked, un-bloodied, as if in peaceful sleep, unmindful of the carnage about him.

The express ground to a sullen halt, the carriages telescoping and buckling, adding to the pile of wreckage, of death and destruction.

And then the fires started. Within a minute the carriages of my train were a blazing inferno, and the shrieks and screams of the men trapped inside seared across the conflagration like the screams of the damned in the fires of Hell. I saw a blackened arm waving in supplication only for it to sink slowly back into the flames. The flames licked hungrily along the smashed carriages. One man, already horribly mangled, lay trapped beneath the wreckage, his mates frantically trying to free him before the flames reached him but to no avail, his screams as the fires consumed him inch by inch echoing across the smoking embankment.

I felt so helpless. Struck dumb and immobile by the sheer scale of the horror around, the dead and the dying, the injured and dazed. The heat from the blazing carriages drove me back, the stench of burning flesh forever in my nostrils.

I saw a medical orderly amputating the leg of a man who had become trapped beneath a mass of metal wheels and bogies, his thin screams virtually unheard amidst the bedlam of dead, dying, and wounded around him. I felt so helpless, I tried to stop an officer as he hurried down the tracks, but he brushed on past me. I felt trapped in an endless nightmare.

Thick black oily smoke blotted out the sky so that only thin wisps of sunlight penetrated the scenes of Hell as the fires raged and consumed. By my feet I found one of the soldier's caps, blood smeared at the brim, and I picked it up, turning it over and over in my hands, the bronze cap badge digging into the flesh of my palm.

The aching weariness swept over me like a tidal wave of despair and hopelessness, and I sank to my knees and leaned back against a telephone pole, the stink of fresh creosote momentarily overcoming the stench of incinerated human flesh. I could take no more and gradually the sounds diminished as my exhaustion, mental and physical, overcame me.

I awoke with a start, back on the Edinburgh train, in my seat in the corner, outside the window there was no death or destruction, no sign of any rail disaster, no broken bodies laid strewn across the trackside. The train was stopped at Gretna Green Station. The little old lady was still there however, and she smiled at me.

'I saw my Donald,' she said, tears sparkling at her eyes, and she then got up and left the train.

I got to Carlisle, badly shaken. Had I been dreaming? I asked one of the delegates at the conference, a local man, had there ever been a train crash locally. He looked at me a bit strangely, 'Oh yes, sometime in 1915 there was a terrible crash near Gretna Green, a troop train carrying a Scots regiment on their way to the front ran into a stationery train and then got hit by an express, the biggest railway disaster in Britain ever, well over two hundred and fifty people killed.'

When I got home, I went to the library and checked, there had indeed been a major rail disaster on May 22nd, 1915 just as the man had said, more than 250 men of the 7th Battalion Royal Scots, Leith Territorial Battalion, died that day, exactly as I had seen,

Did I dream it? Let me just say that the day I travelled from Edinburgh to Carlisle was May 22nd, 1965, exactly fifty years since the disaster.

And I still have in my possession a bloodstained soldiers cap with a ribbon down the back and a bronze cap badge that reads 'The Royal Scots' that I had in my hands when I woke up on the train at Gretna Green.

IT SEEMED LIKE A GOOD IDEA AT THE TIME

It had seemed like a good idea at the time.

We had just come back from a meal at the 'Feathers,' a pretty poor meal it was too, the roast beef was grey and stringy, the mashed potatoes had the consistency of wallpaper paste (roasties not available) the Yorkshire pudding seemed to have been made from ingredients other than flour, eggs, and water (sawdust perhaps), cabbage and broccoli boiled to pulp and the gravy, well don't get me started on the gravy.

The January afternoon was late, and although the sky was a crystal-bright azure, hard grey snow clouds were banking up above the hills at the end of the valley and would soon be upon us. The temperature was below zero and a raw biting wind from the north seared up the valley to freeze our ears and lips.

We hurried on as the wan sun slid inexorably behind the high crags, and darkness crept in.

We were seven, friends from our time at Sheffield University some twelve years ago, where we had all studied with varying degrees of success. I had drifted apart, as happens, and only met up with them again at a university reunion two years ago. Of the others, Keith and Judy were married, as were Dennis and Christine, Bethany, I had not seen since graduating, but we met up again at the reunion and eventually we moved in together, the both of us coming out of long-term failed relationships.

As for Lucy, she was going through a bad time. Her father had recently died, she was in the throes of very bitter divorce, and needed our sympathy and friendship, so we had all agreed to spend a few days cheering her up. Her father had left her a cottage he used to rent out as a summer holiday home, nestled high above the village of Edale in the High Peak of Derbyshire. She thought it would do her good to get away from the disputed marital home in Leeds and her abusive litigious lawyer husband who was fighting to take custody of their two children and deny her access.

Mam Tor scowled down upon us as the dark night set in and the heavy grey snow clouds scudded over, wind driven across the moors.

Bethany and I were edgy together. We had been arguing a lot of late and these few days were make or break, although as far as I could see were sliding towards a gaping chasm. I'd noticed Dennis and Christine were similarly skating carefully around each other. Perhaps in the small confines of the cottage, we were too restricted: tensed, cooped up on top of each other, with hardly any privacy, and nerves stretched taut.

Lucy's rescue mission was turning out to be a trial for us all.

Dennis opened a couple of bottles of an Australian Shiraz he had brought, and we sat desultorily around in the living room, squashed up together on the small settee or perched on the arms of the solitary armchair. Nobody spoke much. Lucy sat withdrawn and taut, nerves still raw, Bethany and I sat together - but not together.

Then the power went out, plunging us into darkness.

'Shit,' someone swore, I felt somebody squeezing by and then a torch beam speared across the room. 'Yes, I thought I'd seen a torch over here earlier,' Keith said, waving it about. 'Candles? Lucy, any candles?'

'I… I'm not sure, in the kitchen cupboard, maybe.'

Keith stumbled into the kitchen and came back with four or five greasy white candles and a box of large barbecue matches and lit the candles before going off again with the torch to check if it was simply that the fuse box had tripped. He came back, shaking his head. 'No, the power seems to be out across the whole valley, I just looked outside.'

Candlelight flickered across our faces, the yellow-orange glow softening lines of tension, and gradually the novelty of the situation began to relax us, and Dennis poured more wine. 'At least we've got plenty of plonk to see us through the dark and stormy night.'

Christine wanted to leave, to go and find a hotel but Dennis would not hear of it, I'd always thought him domineering, and he hadn't much changed. She shrugged and resigned herself to his wishes.

'What shall we do? We can't just sit here all night like dummies,' Christine asked, plaintively.

'Carry on drinking, of course,' Dennis shouted boisterously.

'That's all you'd do anyway,' Christine responded tartly.

Wind rattled at the windows, a sudden keening howl as another storm blast shrieked by, funnelled up the confines of the valley.

'It's really spooky, isn't it, with the wind and storm and candlelight,' Bethany said, in a hushed girly voice which grated on me, but I said nothing.

'Pity it's not Hallowe'en, then it would be really spooky,' Judy added.

'Of ghosts and ghoulies and long-legged beasties and things that go bump in the night,' Keith intoned portentously, and I began to realise that I did not, after all, much like these people.

Throughout it all, Lucy just stared into the night as the candles flickered and wavering and danced across the roughhewn plaster of the walls, deepening shadows where it seemed dark things might lurk, barely glimpsed from the corner of your eye, ready to pounce upon the unwary.

'Somebody draw the curtains,' Bethany asked, 'else I'll be expecting all the while to see some foul creature peering in, you know, like Frankenstein or…'

'Lucy's ex-husband,' Dennis blurted out, well into his cups by now, holding onto another freshly opened bottle of Shiraz as if his life depended on it, and Lucy flinched as if struck.

'Not funny, Dennis,' Christine snapped and went over to put her arms around. Lucy.

'Oh, for God's sake everybody, lighten up. Let's play cards. Or charades. Or something. Anything,' Judy suggested, as ever the peacemaker.

'A séance!' Bethany said unexpectedly. 'I mean, it's spooky and all that. It'll be fun.'

'Fun? I'd have more fun having root canal work!' Dennis again.

'No, that's a really great idea,' Christine enthused. 'Come on, bring the candles, we'll sit round the kitchen table and commune with the spirits.'

'OK, sounds good, I could do with a scotch,' Dennis guffawed, braying dementedly, delighted at his own sense of humour.

We set the candles up in the centre of the round kitchen table, bringing in extra chairs from the dining table. Lucy came along passively, almost catatonic and sat down heavily, staring over our heads.

'Don't we need a weejee board, or whatever you call 'em?' Dennis asked, plonking his glass heavily on the table.

'It's a Ouija board, and no, we don't need one. No, we just hold hands, close our eyes, and ask the spirit guides,' Christine said.

'Don't we need a medium?' Bethany asked.

'Well, that lets me out,' brayed Dennis, 'I'm an extra-large.'

'Extra-large head,' retorted Christine and nobody seemed inclined to disagree.

Lucy suddenly sat up straight. 'I'll be the medium, I've done it before, or at least I've sat in a séance before, and I want to contact Daddy, my father, ask what to do about Howard. I do so miss his advice. He advised me not to marry Howard. God, I should have listened.'

'Good idea, Luce, so how do we go about it?' Keith asked.

'We need more candles, you can't have four or five it has to be three or six or nine. We sit around the table and hold hands and we, I, ask for our spirit guide to join us. Please sit down and hold hands.'

Six candles sat in a ring at the centre of the table, wax trickling down onto a plate.

Keith sat next to Lucy, Christine on the other side of her. I sat down next to Christine and looked for

Bethany to join me, but she waved Judy to sit and sat herself next to Keith, with Dennis between Bethany and Judy. Battle lines drawn it seemed to me.

'Please, all hold hands, close your eyes, and let the spirit move with us.' We sat quietly, relaxed, for about five minutes and then I heard Lucy.

'Oh, beloved father, James Dalton Farmer, we bring you gifts from life into death. Commune with us James Farmer and move among us.' She repeated it again and we sat quietly, waiting. I opened my eyes, candle-shadows danced across the walls, the winds tapped at the window, somewhere a clock ticked, suddenly loud and menacing.

Again, Lucy repeated her mantra.

'Come out, come out wherever you are,' Dennis said in a stage whisper.

'Idiot, you idiot,' Christine snapped sharply. 'You've spoilt it. Again!'

'Shh, shhh,' Lucy whispered, 'I can feel something, a presence.'

Involuntarily I looked around, half expecting some fell creature to ooze out from the deepest shadows.

'Are you with us, beloved spirit?'

We sat still for another five minutes, the tension palpable, every breath audible.

Then I heard the voice, Lucy's mouth was opened as if speaking but it was not her voice.

'Lucy darling, I hear you.' The hairs at the back of my neck rose in chill ripples.

'Daddy?' she asked in her own voice.

'I hear you, my sweetie, just as I always did.'

'Daddy, help me now.'

'How?'

'Howard, tell me what to do about Howard, I'm so sick of it and confused.'

'Say nothing and give him nothing.'

'Is that all?' But he had gone, and other voices came from Lucy's mouth, a Lucy who had now slipped into a deep trance.

A woman's voice said, 'Who is asking the spiritual guides, who is to ask?'

'Is my mother Ok? She passed two years ago, two years ago last June,' Christine asked hesitantly.

'Her name was Alice. She is well, she misses you and loves you, but she is well in the spirit world.'

'Thank you' Christine sobbed.

'David, is there a David?'

'Yes, that's me,' I answered, my heart suddenly hammering.

'Take care of your mother. She is not long to be with you.' That I already knew.

Suddenly Lucy jerked back in her seat, head flung back so that the tendons of her throat stood out like corded ropes, flinging her head from side to side, her hair lashing across her face with every violent spasm. Her legs thrashed against the table legs and one candle fell over, spilling wax across the tabletop.

A growling shriek arced out from her mouth as her whole body began to shake and judder. Christine grabbed her tightly in restraint, Bethany screamed 'Do something do something!'

Keith, sitting next to Lucy, did nothing as if paralysed with fear. The tremors racked her again, and then Lucy gave one last convulsive arched scream and slid to the floor, still in spasm. I leapt up and knelt beside her, forcing open her mouth to check she had not swallowed her tongue. She bit down hard, and I tried to ignore the pain and blood, holding her tongue down to stop her from swallowing it.

Then, as suddenly as it had started, the fit – whatever it was – was over. A thin trickle of sweat ran down from her hair, and across the bridge of her nose. A brightly streaked orange tear in the candlelight. It touched her lips and her tongue slid out to lick it away.

Her eyes opened and she looked around at us, one by one, each gaze intent.

'I saw the Devil,' she said at last, her voice hoarse and rasping 'I saw the Devil.'

'What, what did he look like?' asked Keith hesitantly.

'Like you! And you!' pointing at me, 'And you!' to Bethany, 'And you! And you! Like all of us, the Devil looks like all of us. Like any of us!'

Like any of us!

Lucy seemed calmer for a minute or two as we sat or knelt down beside her, Bethany holding her by the hand.

'Are you all right, Lucy. Do you need a drink?' Dennis asked.

'That's your fucking answer to everything, isn't it?' snapped Christine, 'She needs tea, hot sweet tea.'

'In case you hadn't noticed, darling, the power is off. How are we supposed to make tea, eh, answer me that?'

'It's a gas hob, so we can boil a saucepan of water up in that, make some tea that way,' Christine responded.

'Good idea,' Judy said, 'I think we could all do with a god cup of tea.'

'The universal remedy, eh? How typically British,' Keith, who is Australian, said wryly.

'Thank you. Yes, a cup of tea would be great,' Lucy said. 'David, can you please help me up. I feel a bit unsteady.'

I helped her to her feet, as tottery as a newborn foal. She was pale, very pale and her hair was slick with sweat, but her eyes were bright, and she seemed to be recovering when she suddenly gave out another wild shriek, so highly pitched it was almost beyond human hearing, and she arched back as if her spine was snapped, Further and further she arched back, screaming incoherently, arching so far back her head and shoulders were touching her calves, her spine almost bent in two. Another wild shriek and she dropped to the floor, jerking, and twitching violently, her eyes rolling back into her head.

Then, and I swear that this is true, her body levitated, rising six inches from the floor and she started to spin about the axis of her navel, faster and faster, swirling round and round like a horizontal dervish, her arms and legs flailing helplessly about her. For how long, none of us could afterwards say, it seemed an age but was probably no more than thirty long, long seconds. And then it was if she had been tossed aside, like a petulant child with a fabric doll, and Lucy crashed against the wall, flopping to the floor, loose-limbed and comatose but breathing, albeit shallowly.

Bethany screamed? or was it Judy? Or maybe both. Dennis stood there, mouth open, useless as usual, and it was Keith and I who rushed to Lucy's side.

'Is she…?' asked Judy, fearfully.

No, no, she's breathing. Dennis, call an ambulance, she needs an ambulance, quick,' I shouted.

'The power's down, the phone'll be off.'

'Use your mobile, you fucking idiot.'

'Yeah, right. Mobile. Er, what do I say is wrong with her?'

'Jesus, Dennis, just say she's had a massive fit and is unconscious.'

I vaguely heard him call, concentrating as I was on helping Lucy when her body and limbs began to straighten and stiffen as if there were ropes attached to her ankles and neck, stretching her out. Her muscles went stiff and rigid, as hard set as frozen steak, her head was thrown back and her eyes were open and staring, seeing nothing.

The three girls, Judy, Christine, and Bethany sat on the small sofa, arms around each other, sobbing. Bethany berating herself for having suggested the bloody séance in the first place, every five minutes asking, 'She is going to be all right, isn't she? She is going to be all right, isn't she?'

What could I answer except meaningless platitudes?

Dennis filled his glass again while Keith and I covered poor Lucy with a duvet and sat by her. We were all in shock, saying little, praying for the ambulance to hurry, praying for Lucy's recovery.

Considering the conditions, the ambulance arrived quickly, no more than forty or forty-five minutes. The paramedics checked Lucy's vital functions and lifted her onto a stretcher, although they could probably have carried her out without it, Lucy being so stiff.

'What's wrong with her?' pleaded Bethany. 'She'll be all right, won't she?'

''Not sure, love,' answered the paramedic. 'Could be hypertonia, won't know for sure 'til we get her to hospital, Sheffield Northern General most likely, and the doctors can check her out more fully.'

To cut a long story short, little physical evidence

could be found for Lucy's condition. CT scans revealed no lesions to the basal ganglia, spinal cord injury, a stroke, or cerebral palsy, all possible causes of her muscular rigidity and catatonia. She was not epileptic. The muscular rigidity slowly eased, and Lucy recovered the use of her limbs, but remained in a catatonic state for several weeks, weeks in which Howard, her bastard of her husband, got into court and obtained custody of their children, but really, what other option was available?

Learned consultants now considered her condition to be a severe mental disorder and she was transferred initially to the Psychiatric Department at the Northern General and then to a specialist ward at the Michael Carlisle Centre. Of course, we visited her there, but she seemed not to recognise who any of us were. Dennis remains a prat of course, and Christine has left him, good for her. Judy and Keith are still together, their relationship somehow strengthened by the ordeal and are planning to live in Australia and I can't say as I blame them. Bethany and I split soon afterwards, but hey, shit happens, you know.

Poor Lucy, lost in her own demon inhabited world, never did recover. Then exactly one year after the night of the séance, she found her way out of the ward and onto the road, waited for a heavy lorry to come down the hill at speed, stepped out in front of it and was killed instantly.

Like I said, the séance seemed like a good idea at the time, but the awful consequences.

The awful, awful consequences!

FOOTSTEPS

Charlotte, known as Charlie, finally admitted to herself that her life was a mess.

Alan, her husband of seven years had gone off with a woman twelve years older than her, ouch, and the divorce proceedings were getting ugly. She had just lost her driving licence, too many drinks at a party, her cat Furball had been run over, she had fallen out with her best friend Angie over a silly quarrel, and her career as a university lecturer had stalled, having twice been overlooked for promotion.

Charlie realised she needed to get away and get her head together and maybe, finally, complete her PhD doctoral thesis. A doctorate could give her career a boost and restore some self-confidence.

Somewhere with peace and quiet and no distractions and Charlie thought she had found the ideal solution. Alder House was a mid-Victorian former rectory in the depths of the Peak District, now operating as a writer's retreat. *Sounds perfect,* thought Charlie and as it was the Easter break, she booked herself in for three weeks. 'Should be long enough. The research is done, most of the chapters are written in draft, so three solid weeks should complete the rest ready for a final edit.'

Charlie set off for Alder House with a much lighter heart than she had felt for many months.

It was strangely quiet in the house as she rang the bell on the reception desk and a grey-haired, middle-aged woman emerged from the back of house. 'Yes. May I help you?'

'I have a reservation, Charlotte Gatehouse?'

'Oh yes, so I see, Miss Gatehouse, is it?' she asked, looking at Charlie's now naked ring finger.

'Yes… er… no, Mrs, but Charlie will do.'

'I am Mrs Sexton, the manager. I've put you in room six, if you would follow me.'

'Thank you. It seems very quiet, are there many other guests?'

'Not at the moment. In fact, you are the only guest at present.'

'The only guest? But this is Easter. I expected it to be busy, full even.'

'I'm sure other guests will arrive… eventually. Here we are, Mrs Gatehouse, this is your room. I hope you will be comfortable. Dinner is served at seven, please do not be late.'

'Yes, I mean no, of course.'

The room was adequately furnished, rather colourless but gleamingly clean and whatever shortcomings the room might have was compensated by the magnificent view, green hills and moors rolling across the Edale valley and up towards Mam Tor. She opened the window and took a deep breath; the air was fresh and invigorating.

'I shall do rather well here, I think,' she said aloud

and setting up her laptop, consulted her research notes, and got to work.

Dinner that evening was rather insipid: tinned tomato soup, boiled gammon steak, boiled potatoes, and peas with tinned peaches and ice cream for dessert.

'Is there a bar? she asked, 'No bar,' replied Mrs Sexton, 'but I can get you a drink.'

Charlie was disappointed. Although she was there to work, she had anticipated lively discussions with other guests around a bar in the evenings. She asked for a gin and tonic, but it was weak, with warm tonic water, but, nevertheless, she'd had a productive afternoon on her thesis and was not too dissatisfied. After another weak G & T, Charlie went back to her room.

It was 2:39 a.m. when something woke her up; she could hear footsteps, heavy footsteps coming from the adjacent room, room five. *Another guest, moving in,* she thought. The footsteps then came out of the bedroom, onto the corridor and over to her door. Charlie could hear movement outside, so she quickly switched on the bedside lamp, and fearfully watched the door handle. The footsteps then moved away and back into room five. It was a long time before she got back to sleep.

At breakfast she was surprised that she was still the only guest. 'Has another guest moved into room five?' she asked Mrs Sexton.

'Room five? No, indeed not, Mrs Gatehouse, room five is not occupied and has not been for some time.'

Strange, thought Charlie, convinced she had heard something, *Maybe I dreamt it,* but a niggling worm of disquiet encircled her heart, and she found concentration on her thesis difficult.

Dinner that evening was again disappointing: tinned

mushroom soup, boiled haddock, frozen chips, and peas with tinned pineapple and cream as dessert. Rather than a G & T, Charlie asked for a glass of white wine, 'Chardonnay if you have it.'

'Only house white,' replied Mrs Sexton. The wine was sharp, with a sour aftertaste. Charlie decided against another glass and asked for a whisky instead. It was palatable but barely a teaspoon in quantity.

It was 2:39 a.m. when she again woke up to the sound of footsteps coming from room five over to her own door. Charlie sat up in bed, breathing heavily, fearful, her heart pounding fiercely. She stared at the door, expecting it to burst open and that she would be attacked and raped. Or worse! But as on the previous night the footsteps then retreated back to room five. Charlie began to breathe more evenly, and the fear she felt turned to anger.

'I'm going to get to the bottom of this,' she vowed. There would be strong words with Mrs Sexton in the morning. Of that there was no doubt.

'Mrs Sexton, I definitely heard someone in room five last night, now, just what is going on?' Charlie demanded angrily as soon as she got downstairs.

'Room five? I told you Mrs Gatehouse, room five is unoccupied.'

'I heard someone.'

'There is no one. How many more times must I tell you?'

'Show me then. Show me inside room five.'

'Very well, if you insist,' Mrs Sexton replied, taking the key to room five from its pigeonhole behind the reception desk. 'There, as I told you' she said, once the door was opened. There was no bedding on the bed, no clothes in the wardrobe, no personal belongings at the bedside or on the desk by the window. 'As you can see, this room is not occupied nor has it been for some time.'

'But I heard something,' Charlie insisted.

'This is a very old building, and it creaks and groans, so that is most likely what you heard. If indeed you heard anything at all'

There was little more that Charlie could do or say, but she was far from satisfied as there was no doubt in her mind that she had heard something. After breakfast she took herself off for long walk across the valley, but even glorious scenery and a clean fresh breeze could do little to disperse her unease about Alder House and room five. The sound of those footsteps echoed and re-echoed through her head. She managed little in the way of work on her thesis that afternoon.

Once again it was 2:39 when the heavy menacing footsteps came to her door. Her heart pounded again, her breathing rapid and stressed, but after what seemed an age the footsteps finally retreated back into room five.

'I've had enough of this' Charlie swore and gathering the duvet about herself, she quickly ran downstairs and into the lounge. She sat on a sofa and huddled herself into the duvet to wait for the morning when she would get out of Alder House as soon as she could, never to return.

But then, to her horror she heard footsteps, those heavy menacing footsteps coming down the stairs. 'No! No! No!' she screamed inwardly as a blackened, shadowy form emerged from the foot of the stairs. She ran to the front door; she would run out into the night as she was to get away from… whatever nightmare creature it was.

She wrenched open the door, only to face a hideous apparition, tall and hooded, with no visible face except glaring yellow eyes as a skeletal hand reached out and seized her by the throat.

With a scream of terror… Charlie woke to find herself in a tangle of sweat-soaked sheets, with a hammering heart and strident rapid breathing. It was 2:39 a.m. She dashed to the bathroom to be violently sick then washed her face in cold water, staring at her fear-ravaged face in the mirror. Once her breathing had returned to normal, she showered, dressed, packed her bags, and as soon as Mrs Sexton was about in the morning, Charlie checked out.

'There can be no refund, Mrs Gatehouse, our conditions are quite clear on that point.'

'I don't care about a bloody refund, just order me a taxi.'

Charlie felt too stressed to wait for a train at the local station and so took the taxi all the way to her home in Sheffield. It was expensive, but she considered it worth every penny.

As she carried her bags into the house, she felt again how lonely it seemed, echoingly silent ever since Alan had walked out. As she unpacked her bags, Charlie realised that she had left a pair of her favourite earrings on the bedside table of her room in Alder House. They were from India, little triangles of gold skilfully wired together to form a larger triangle, handed down from her great-grandmother whose husband had been a District Officer in Peshawar.

'Bugger,' she swore. 'I'll ring that cow Mrs Sexton, and ask her to post them on, no way am I ever going back there again.'

She went shopping to stock up on food, there being

nothing in the fridge. Then she went back upstairs to fetch her laptop and her heart gave a lurch. There, on the bedside were the earrings. Definitely, most definitely they had not been there earlier. They had been left at Alder House. With an ice-cold tremor of fear running through her veins, Charlie searched through every room in the house but found nothing, Nobody.

That night, before she went to bed, Charlie double checked that the front door was locked and bolted and all windows firmly shut.

It was 2:39 a.m. when she awoke to hear ominous, menacing footsteps coming up the stairs to her bedroom.

She was no longer alone in her house.

JACK THE RIPPER, MYSTERY SOLVED!

I suppose to you it looks just like an ordinary egg timer sitting there on my kitchen worktop. You know, the glass tube, pinched to a narrow waist at the centre, half full of sand, set within a polished wooden frame and when turned upside down the sand runs through from the top half to the bottom and when all the sand has run through, your boiled egg is ready?

Yours might be - but mine is actually a time machine. A genuine time machine that can transport me anywhere in place and time. I could not for one minute explain how it works, something to do with quantum physics, quarks, nuclear particle fission and an extremely complex scientific process called ACTIMORASTIFLORE, don't begin to ask me what the acronym ACTIMORASTIFLORE stands for, it sounds like an ingredient in toothpaste (for brighter smiles use Glow White Toothpaste with super dynamic ACTIMORASTIFLORE) but it isn't, it's what makes a time machine work. Anti-matter maybe?

Whatever. It works. There is also quite a complex program involved in setting the destination place, date and time. I have to key into my laptop where and when

I want to go and it prints out the sequence of turns of the glass tube required to set the date. So many turns clockwise, so many anti-clockwise, half turns, quarter turns, it can be really laborious and if I get it wrong, it causes all sorts of problems!

For instance, the last time I time travelled, I programmed it to go back to 1966 and the Soccer World Cup. I wanted to see England beat West Germany in the Final at Wembley. I must have made too many clockwise turns because I ended up in London in 1666, right in the middle of the Great Fire of London. I got my eyebrows scorched that day, I can tell you, mind you it was quite something to see the old St Paul's Cathedral go up in smoke.

I'm planning another trip. You see, I have this brilliant idea. To go back in time and solve the world's great mysteries! Like, why did the dinosaurs die out or how did the Pharaohs build the Great Pyramids, or who was with Marilyn Monroe the night she died and who killed JFK? Think about it, I can transport myself to the Texas Book Depository in Dallas on November 22nd, 1964 and see whether Lee Harvey Oswald really did fire those fatal shots or not, and if not he, then who did?

Or, and this is the one I'm working on at the moment, who was Jack the Ripper? Imagine, the greatest murder mystery of all time. To go back to those dark, fear-ridden streets of Whitechapel in London's East End in 1888 and see exactly who Jack the Ripper was. Not that I can prevent him from carrying out his ghastly crimes, time travel does not permit you to make any changes, you can only observe from a sort of time-warp bubble. You are there, physically there, but you cannot interfere or interact with anybody or anything. But there is nothing to stop me taking a photograph and from that photograph identify the killer.

So, we know when and where the notorious murderer struck, we know who his victims were but despite the most intensive research ever carried out into any crime anywhere in the world, nobody can say for certain just who Jack the Ripper was. I intend to be to put that right, by being there, at the spot, at the time, camera at the ready. Is there a danger to me? No, in the same way that I cannot interact with persons there, by the same token they cannot interact with me. Or, at least that's the theory. I think not! I hope not! Being confronted by the most infamous murderer in history, bloody knives in hand, is not a pleasant thought if the theory proves to be wrong.

In the early hours of November 9th, 1888, Jack the Ripper committed his most brutal killing, strangling and then mutilating the body of Mary Kelly in the most hideous manner possible. I intend to be there, at No 13 Millers Court, 26 Dorset Street as Jack completes his bloody work and leaves the dingy room where Mary Kelly practiced her trade. It will be the scoop of the year, of the century. Book deals. Television chat shows. Fame! Money! All will be mine!

I key the details into my laptop: early hours, November 9, 1888. No. 26 Dorset Street., London's East End. As always it took time for the complex parameters of time, place, motion and ACTIMORASTIFLORE to calculate the program. I printed it out. Altogether it would take 213 different turns and inversions to complete the time travel input program into the machine.

A tired wrist later, the turns were complete. I

packed my new digital camera into a small backpack and, holding tight onto the timer, inverted it for the final time.

Imagine the biggest big dipper you have ever been on or seen, multiply that by a thousand, a million. Imagine yourself inside a kaleidoscope on this giant big dipper, twisting and spiralling, cascading downwards in a fantastic fusion of flashing light and sound that sears the back of your eyes in a blaze of fluorescent colour. And then, a sudden stop that leaves your stomach several miles away as you arrive at your destination. Sometimes I feel nauseous for hours afterwards. After a minute or two to recover my breath, my legs were still a bit shaky as well, I packed the timer away in a special lined box in my backpack, (if it gets broken on a journey, you are in big, big, trouble with no means of getting back to your own time). You would also notice that the sand is trickling through a single grain at a time, so slowly you would hardly notice it but once the last grain has fallen through, whoosh, back you go to your own time but four and a half minutes later.

I looked around me and there I was! The East End of London, November 9th, 1888. Dorset Street. It is night, cold, and slithering fingers of fog creep along the rain-sodden, broken-paved streets. I pull my jacket closer about me. Foolishly, I had forgotten to put on a coat and the cold dank air, reeking as it did of rotting garbage, raw sewage, and of a swollen dead rat the size of a cat that lay in the gutter by my feet, shivered into my bones. The guttering gas light gave little illumination and the thickening mist coalesced in the dark corners so that the street pressed in even narrower still.

Jack the Ripper, the Whitechapel murderer killed four or five street women, slashing and mutilating, removing bodily organs. His final victim before disappearing forever into the legends of crime was Mary Kelly, killed and mutilated this very night. At this very spot!

The fog swirled in tighter, shrouding me in clammy mists, so thick I could taste the coal fumes and soot. A carriage clattered past, throwing up spumes of water from the puddles. I could hear shouts in the distance, muffled by the fog, drunken laughter and then a cry of 'Oh, murder,' but I could not tell from which direction as the thick swirling fog distorted the sounds. My heart beat furiously as I crept into the narrow alley into Millers Court. I knew that Mary Kelly's room was on the ground floor, to the right of the narrow passage. Was the Ripper already there, carrying out his ghastly work? I took out my camera, set it for flash with red eye reduction and slowly crept on, hearing my footsteps echoing back from the fog.

From my research I knew that that there was a broken pane in Mary Kelly's window, a thin, ragged piece of material hanging there as a curtain. Suddenly emboldened, I crept forward further into the gloomy fog-smeared alleyway. A cat arched its back, spat at me, and ran past, brushing against my leg as it did so. A gas lamp at the far end of Millers Court was the only light, gruel-thin light which barely penetrated the miasmic murk. Barely able to breathe I crept further forward, the door to No 13 was there, next to it the window with the broken pane. I listened, straining my ears, but could hear nothing. Another muffled shout from across the courtyard, a scurry of rats nearby, and silence again. Thick tendrils of fog curled about my feet. I shivered violently with cold – or was it fear, my stomach knotted and roiled with tension. Why was I doing this? I peered through the broken pane of the window, a single candle guttered inside but I could see nothing, then a shadow suddenly sped across the window like a phantom and startled I stepped back, my heart beating fit to burst.

Suddenly the door opened. A tall man stepped out and peered warily about him, his coat collar was turned up and his hat was pulled down to cover as much of his face as possible. I raised the camera, ready to shoot when suddenly he turned, saw me, and with a snarl sprang towards me. I saw the knife in his hand, raised ready to strike.

The last grain of sand fell through the timer.

My egg is ready, boiled to perfection, the yolk buttery yellow and runny, the white firm and smooth. Perfect.

What? You didn't really believe my egg timer was a time machine, did you?

DANNY BLACKWOOD, CHAMPION OF THE WORLD

The lift glided smoothly to a halt, the doors slid open, and Danny Blackwood stepped out into the lobby, a large pyramidal atrium, some five or six stories high. From the centre of the atrium hung a vast crystal chandelier, dazzlingly diamond-bright, beneath which a small fountain clad in blue and white Turkish tiles delicately played. The gentle splash of water was softly sibilant, soothing, and somehow reassuring. The floor of the atrium was laid with white Carrara marble, polished to a mirror-like sheen and tall floral arrangements, smelling sweetly of rose and lily and jasmine gently permeating the air, were set on marble stands at intervals around the perimeter of the lobby. Soft music played and Danny thought he recognised Górecki's Symphony #3, the 'Symphony for Sorrowful Souls,' but he could not be certain.

Looking around, as if not quite sure where he was, Danny could see soft armchairs and plush leather sofas clustered around coffee tables on which were more flowers arrayed in crystals vases. To the far side there was what appeared to be a reception desk, from which a receptionist was beckoning him over, giving him a beaming smile as he approached.

'Good afternoon, Mr Blackwood. We have been expecting you.'

'Expecting me?' he answered, somewhat confused.

'Yes, indeed, we have had your reservation for some time now.'

'Reservation? I'm sorry, this might sound like a stupid question, but where exactly are we?'

'No need to apologise, Mr Blackwood, you've had a long and tiring journey, and naturally must be feeling a bit disorientated. Many of our guests feel the same, but in answer to your question, we are in the headquarters building of the Nicholas Old Corporation.'

'Nicholas Old Corporation? An office block building, I thought it was a hotel, especially when you said that I had a reservation?'

'Oh, but our guests do stay here. All the time.'

'I… just don't…'

The receptionist, whose name badge he could now read as Selene, gave him another beaming smile. 'Please, Mr Blackwood, you do look so tired, just take a seat over here, I'm sure the manager will be here shortly, and he can answer all your questions and explain the situation more fully,' she said, pointing to a nearby sofa and magazine-strewn coffee table.

Danny sank gratefully into the soft brown leather, smelling faintly of lemon polish, of the indicated sofa. He leant back, closed his eyes, and let the weariness wash over him. He was so, so tired but even so, he still tried to sort out all the thoughts raging through his brain.

The Nicholas Old Corporation? He had no recollection of any dealings or even contact with any company by that name. If it came to it, he had no clear recollections of anything that had happened over the past few days. All he knew was that he was in a strange place that he had never heard of and no idea how he had got there, except by the lift he had exited some minutes ago.

Danny Blackwood was a racing driver. A top-rated Formula One driver with twenty-two Grand Prix victories to his name, but to his intense disappointment and frustration, no drivers' championships. Other drivers, lesser drivers to his mind, had won championships with far fewer race wins to their name and it rankled, Jesus, how it rankled.

To add insult to injury, over the past four seasons he had been runner-up twice and third twice, losing out last season to one of the 'lesser' drivers when leading in the final race and on the way to the drivers' title when a bungled pit stop resulted in the loss of a wheel and the end of his race, the end of a sure win and most galling of all, the end to his championship.

This season, he was again leading on points with seven race wins and only needed to finish ahead of his two nearest challengers in the final race in Brazil to be champion. Twice the drivers' championship had been in his grasp only for it to be snatched away at the last minute. It was not going to happen again, whatever it took, it was not going to happen again. He was going to be world champion, just had to be, nothing else smattered, nor ever would. No matter what it took, he was going to be the champion of the world. Just had to be.

A man could sell his soul for that.

However, no matter how hard he tried, he simply could not relate to his present circumstances. What exactly was he doing here? And exactly, who, or what was the Nicholas Old Corporation? Another wave of tiredness swept over him and he let his thoughts drift away and began to doze.

'Mr Blackwood, so very good to see you again.' The deep resonant voice of a man intruded abruptly into his doze, jerking him back from the depths with a shock that set his heart pounding. Before him stood a tall man, 6'3" or 6'4" in height, slim, aristocratically elegant, of indeterminate age, anything between forty-five and sixty-five with swept back silver hair that came to a sharp widow's peak on a high forehead, hair so silver that it seemed to shimmer in the light. He had a pointed, silver, goatee beard and was dressed in an expensive light-grey mohair suit, white shirt, plain red tie, and highly polished black oxford shoes.

'Shit man, you gave me quite a start there,' Danny said sharply. 'I was just having a few zzzzs and didn't hear you come over.'

'Sorry about that, I was tempted to let you sleep on, but I do have a busy schedule and need to get on, so do please excuse me.'

The man smiled thinly but it was a smile which did not quite reach his eyes, eyes that were disconcertingly black and flecked with gold, with thin arched eyebrows that almost met in the middle above his sharp patrician nose.

'Yeah, well, I do need to get to know what the hell is going on here and what I'm supposed to be doing, I mean, what is this place?

'Please come with me. My office is just here, and all will be explained.'

Wearily Danny got to his feet and followed the tall man, every footstep leaden with the effort.

'Please, Danny. May I call you Danny? Please take

a seat,' he said, ushering Danny into his office, a large brightly lit room in muted neutral colours but with many pictures, modern art mostly, hanging on the walls. Danny thought he recognised a Picasso, a Rothko, and a pair of Jackson Pollack's amongst many others and was surprised that when he looked closely, the pictures were originals. *There must be an absolute bloody fortune hanging on these walls,* he thought, *Whatever this Nicholas Old Corporation does, it obviously does it very successfully. Maybe that's why I'm here. They're an investment group, that's it, they want me to invest with them, well, I'll see what they've got to say.*

'I see you're admiring my little collection. Many of my… clients feel constrained to make them available to me, at a discounted cost of course.' The thin humourless smile crept across his face again.

'You said it was good to see me again,' Danny said as he sat down. 'We've met before? Only I don't recall…'

'Oh yes, only very recently.'

'I still don't…'

'Let me refresh your memory, I am Nicholas Old, the Chairman and CEO of this… enterprise?'

'Nicholas Old? No sorry, I still don't recognise you… or recall how and why we met.'

'Try transposing my name, Nicholas Old, Old Nicholas. And use the diminutive.'

'The diminutive?'

'Shortening the name, Danny, shortening it.'

'Old Nicholas… Old Nicholas. Old Nick!' A torrent of ice-cold horror flooded through his bones, and his heart began to palpitate so fiercely with terror he thought it was about to burst as dread-sweat spurted about his head and neck. He could barely take a breath, his lungs clogged with gelid fear and his stomach knotted and roiled as hot acrid vomit surged up to his gorge. He felt as though he was spinning into a vortex of fright-black dread. He was close to fainting, slumping deeper into his chair as the room seemed to revolve around in a dizzying blur.

'You, the Devil, Satan! How? How, did... I... the Devil?' he gasped in terror-taut snatches.

'Indeed, I am so called, amongst many other names.'

Danny's brain was a mush of confused, disorientated fear, he could not think or rationalise, as though his head was about to explode, to splatter blood and brain matter across the walls in an obscene parody of the artwork.

'How... this place? I... just don't, don't... understand... please.'

'You are confused, naturally so. So please allow me then to elucidate. I am, as you surmise Old Nick, sometimes called Lucifer, or Mephistopheles, Satan, or any other diabolic name you care to mention, they are many and manifold and you are, as you probably also surmise, at the threshold of what is popularly known as Hell, also known in various cultures as Gehenna, Hades, Diyu, Naraka, or Purgatory. Many names, so many names, all meaning the same thing. Personally, I simply call it home.'

Danny's sensations of dread and terror intensified as nausea again seared his stomach and gorge, his hands shaking and his heart, if possible, seeming to race ever more fiercely.

'How... I... why?'

'Please don't interrupt me, Danny, I find it discourteous.'

'Sorry... I... yeah, sorry.'

'As I was saying, you are, to put it simply, in Hell and will shortly pass through the Gates of Eternal Torment to the Ten Courts of Hell which will ultimately decide your fate.'

Danny was about to interrupt once more before a raised finger from the Devil halted him as another sudden surge of fear raged through his body.

'You, Danny, as you will shortly recall, called on me for my help, in return for your soul, you asked me to ensure that you become the Formula One Drivers Champion. I have kept my promise and am now collecting my dues.'

'But the race, the race in Brazil,' Danny could not help himself from interjecting again.

'Ah, yes, the race in Brazil, how very tragic! It was the worst accident in Grand Prix history, when all three contenders for the title were, regretfully, killed in a fiery multi car crash. Danny Blackwood, as promised, you are the Champion of the World, albeit, like the late Jochen Rindt, a posthumous one.'

DEAR MRS. BURTON

'Dead Mrs. Burton,'

I refer to your letter of the 18th July, but really don't know how to respond to you.'

I looked up at the monitor.

I had typed Dead Mrs. Burton.

Easily done, the D and R are close to each other on the keyboard, the R on the top line and the D on the second line, almost immediately below, and I am not a very accomplished typist. Easily done.

I shifted the cursor and made the correction.

Dear Mrs. Burton.

I refer to your letter of the 18th July, but really don't know how to respond to you. If you truly believe that your husband is trying to kill you, then this is very much a matter for the police, rather than a private investigator.

I looked at Mrs. Burton's letter again. In it she claimed that her husband Eric had tried to kill her on at least three separate occasions. On the first occasion he had tried (so she said) to push her over the cliff at Beachy Head whilst they were on a day trip to the Sussex Coast. He appeared to stumble over a protecting stone and fell heavily into her, almost causing her to go over the edge. As she whirled and windmilled her arms to try and gain her balance, Eric made no attempt to help her. He merely looked around to see if anyone else was about. Fortunately, an elderly couple were walking a Springer spaniel not so far away, else, Mrs. Burton now believes, he would have pushed her again. As it was, she dropped to her knees and saved herself from going over. She had accepted his version of events at the time, that he had not realised she was in danger, which was why he had not helped her.

I looked at the monitor again.

Dead Mrs. Burton it read again, but I was certain I had made the correction. Certain!

I corrected it again, this time making absolutely sure that I altered the D into an R.

Dear Mrs. Burton,

I refer to your letter...

How do you respond to a letter from someone who is convinced her husband is trying to kill her? Who won't go to the police because she thinks they will not believe her? She had written - 'I have twice been hospitalised following nervous breakdowns and I am sure that anything I say about my husband will be dismissed as further evidence of mental instability.'

On the second occasion that she claims he tried to kill her, Eric had insisted on ordering a Chinese takeaway for dinner, even though she had already prepared a vegetable lasagne. He went to collect the takeaway himself, even though the 'Golden Dragon' on East Street normally delivered. He did not eat any of the Szechwan Beef Chilli, normally one of his favourite dishes. Afterwards she felt violently ill, almost to the point of unconsciousness, but Eric refused to call a doctor or ambulance.

It was only by drinking heavily salted water that she was able to vomit and empty her stomach. It was this incident, taken together with the cliff side 'accident,' which aroused her suspicions that he might be trying to murder her. – 'A horrible suspicion for any wife to have about her husband. It was also about this time that I discovered my husband was being unfaithful, that he had a girlfriend. I know who she is. She works in his office as Assistant Export Manager and is married herself. Marilyn Croft, the bitch.'

I looked at the screen again, wondering what else I could say to her. The hairs on the back of my neck began to rise and I felt a chill ripple through me like an Arctic wind.

It read: Dead Mrs. Burton.

I felt as though I had been punched in the solar plexus. There could be no mistake this time, I had most definitely, without any possibility of doubt, typed Dear rather than Dead. But there it was on the screen again. Dead Mrs. Burton.

My hand shook as I picked up Mrs. Burton's letter. I dialled the telephone number printed on the letter head, but it just rang and rang and rang without answer. So, I was no wiser than I had been before.

Words began to scroll down the monitor:

Dead Mrs. Burton

Dead Mrs. Burton

Dead Mrs. Burton

Dead Mrs. Burton

Dead Mrs. Burton

Dead Mrs. Burton

Dead Mrs. Burton

Dead Mrs. Burton

DEAD MRS. BURTON.

I was afraid, I can tell you. Seriously afraid. Seriously spooked.

Reaching down below my desk, I switched off the power to my computer without even saving or closing down the program. It meant I would have to reboot when I switched on again, but I was so shaken I had reacted without thinking, anxious only to clear the screen of those awful words.

A virus, it had to be a virus, somebody had infected my computer with a virus that garbled up everything you type. That was it. It had to be. Didn't it?

I went and made myself a cup of coffee to calm my nerves, and then read the final paragraphs of Mrs. Burton's letter:

'I became so paranoid about my fears that Eric was trying to kill me that I almost stopped eating, certainly anything that he had prepared or brought in. I was afraid to go to sleep at night in case he tried to smother me with a pillow – to say that I am a nervous wreck is a great understatement. On the third occasion I am sure that he had tried to kill me, Eric rewired my hairdryer, I don't know exactly what he did, as I am not mechanically minded, but when I tried to use it, I got a tremendous electric shock and if I had not been wearing my trainers – with rubber soles- I would surely have died.

Eric rushed in, saw me still alive but in shock, unplugged the dryer and took it away. I can only assume he corrected whatever he had done to make it unsafe. I cannot go to the police with this, so I am asking you, as a last resort to help, to prove that Eric is trying to kill me. You are my last hope.

Please!

Please!

Valerie Burton

But what could I do?

After some time, I switched the computer back on and rebooted it. The letter I had started to write had deleted, of course, but I called up the word processing program and began again, more than a little apprehensive.

Dear Mrs Burton,

I refer to your letter of the 18th July – more than a month since I had received the letter and I felt a terrible knot of guilt hardening like hot concrete in my stomach. Why had I waited so long before responding? The answer I suppose is that I did not believe her story, just as she feared that the police would not believe her. Even so, the desperation of her fear was so evident in her letter and I had ignored her pleas for help. But what could I have done? I asked myself, trying to assuage my conscience. Take the letter to the police myself? Possibly they might have investigated but I rather doubt it, far too busy putting up speed cameras everywhere.

I tried to ignore the letter, tried to ignore my response. I turned away from the screen and took my cup out to the kitchen to wash it out. Then I took the rubbish sack out to the dustbin, desperate to find excuses not to go back to the computer. I had a cigarette, feeling the warm sun on my face, but then I could avoid it no longer.

I sat down at my desk again, turning my head away, trying not to look at the glowing monitor screen, my heart hammering wildly as I typed again those dread words... Dear Mrs Burton. I turned away once more and closed my eyes, steeling myself to look at the screen again.

Slowly I turned towards the screen, my heart hammering in fearful anticipation. I let out a mighty sigh of relief as I read what I had typed.

Dear Mrs. Burton it read. Dear not Dead. It must have been a virus before, when I've finished, I'll run the virus guard program again and get rid of whatever it was.

Just then I heard the letter box rattle. It was the free weekly local newspaper, delivered by a cocky schoolboy called Terry Wickes who thought he deserved not only a Christmas tip but an Easter, Eid, Diwali, and Passover tips as well.

Casually I unfolded the paper. HOLIDAY TRAGEDY ran the headline and with another searing sense of dread I read on. Tragedy struck a local couple's idyllic Silver Wedding holiday in Corfu when Valerie Burton, aged forty-six, drowned whilst swimming in their hotel swimming pool. Mrs. Burton's husband Eric stated that his wife had gone for a late-night dip by herself. 'We had had a lovely meal and a few glasses of retsina and a brandy or two at the local taverna, I had no idea Valerie was going to the pool as I had fallen asleep in the chair as soon as we got back to our room...

I ran back to the computer.

Words were scrolling down the screen.

SOMETIMES YOU JUST KILL THE WRONG PEOPLE

Dead Mrs Burton
Dead Mrs Burton
Dead Mrs Burton
Dead Mrs. Burton.
DEAD MRS. BURTON!!!!!!!!!

THE CHINESE HAT BOX

I don't believe in ghosts.

Or at least, that's what I used to say.

Let me tell you a thing or two I've learned about ghosts.

1: They are very scary.

2: They don't just haunt old Victorian mansions with creaky wooden floors.

3: They are very, very scary.

It happened like this.

I recently moved into a new apartment: two bedrooms, bathroom, kitchen, and lounge/diner, with a balcony offering a grandstand vista of the dual carriageway and endless miles of rush hour traffic. Compact was the word used by the estate agent - which is estate-agentese for shoebox-sized.

My fiancée, Sadie, and I had planned to move in together - but twelve days before the move, she went off with Rob, the estate agent who sold it to us.

I've always hated people called Rob - and estate agents.

We had planned a minimalist approach to the furnishing, not because of artistic ideals but due to a minimalist budget. However, one thing we did buy from a local antique-boutique, (estate-agentese for small junk shop) was a lacquered Chinese box which now stood in the corner of the lounge.

The box, lacquered a glossy black, was a perfect cube about fifteen inches in size. The large hinges were golden brass, elaborately patterned with a swirling dragon pattern, as was the face plate of the keyhole. Chinese writing in red was painted onto the lid.

Sadie had found a nice, black-glazed, round vase to sit on top of the box and hold dried flowers or twigs. Unfortunately, the vase had got broken. She'd thrown it at me as a parting gift on her way to be with Rob. Shame, I liked that vase.

The box intrigued me. What was its purpose? More importantly, what was inside it? Did it contain fabulous artefacts, a hidden treasure map – or some very old tea leaves? I rattled the box about, there was definitely something inside but whatever it was, it was not very heavy. Maybe it was a hatbox. I just had to open it.

As there was no key, I needed a picklock and I didn't think a bent pin was going to do the trick. I found a bunch of Allen keys, and after oiling the innards of the lock with olive oil (light extra virgin) I eased the L-shaped end of the medium sized Allen key into the lock and began to work it around, feeling for the pins. After a while my fingers ached, the key was slippery with oil and I had to use pliers to get a better grip. For two nights I fiddled about with that lock and had almost given up when, with a soft brassy click, the key turned, and the lock opened.

Feeling a sudden trepidation, I held my breath as I slowly eased the lid open, a faint smell of corruption seeping from the box as I did so. I peered inside. A crimson silk bag almost filled the box, and slowly I lifted it out. The neck of the bag was tightly tied with silk cord which took me some minutes to untie. Inside the bag was a scroll of parchment and a round object wrapped in more crimson silk. Unrolling the parchment, I saw it was covered in Chinese calligraphy with an elaborately carved red chop or seal stamped at the bottom.

I then unwrapped the object and almost fell of my chair when I saw what it was. A yellowed human skull. It wasn't a hatbox, it was a head box!

A sudden shiver ran down my spine. I did not want this thing in my house. I carefully wrapped up the head again and placed it back into the bag and then into the box, closing the lid rather too hurriedly so that it cracked like a gunshot, making me jump. I was suddenly feeling very jittery. I looked at the scroll again, the parchment crackling under my fingers like tomb-dried skin. I don't know what the writing meant, but I doubt it was the takeaway menu from the 'Peking Restaurant'

Another shiver ran through me like an icicle spear. *Get a grip*, I told myself, *it's nothing but an old skull, somebody probably put it in the box for a joke.* But deep inside I knew it wasn't, so I tried to lock the box again, but the Allen key refused to catch on the pins. I wasn't going to leave that lid unfastened, so I tied it down tightly with string.

The chill seeped through my bones and I huddled deeper under the duvet, wrapping it tightly about me. The night was dark, so dark it was as though the bedroom had been shrouded in black iced-velvet, excluding all light. The hairs on the back of my neck began to rise and my heart pumped furiously with fear as I could sense somebody – something- in the room.

'Who's there?' I called. 'What do you want?' I reached for the bedside lamp and switched it on. Only a thin glimmer of light oozed from the bulb, as if all the luminescence had drained away. The gruel-thin light barely penetrated to the corners of the room, but I could see nothing there.

Shivering with cold and dread, I slid out of bed and made my way into the main room. Again, nobody there but the awful sense of another presence would not leave me sitting heavily in my stomach like a churning avalanche. I searched every room – checked on the balcony and out into the communal entrance lobby. Nothing!

Still feeling very uneasy I made my way back towards the bedroom, and it was only then that I noticed that the string around the box had become untied and the lid of the box was open! If I was frightened before, it was nothing compared to the terror I felt now. Rushing over to the box I slammed it shut and piled on as many books as I could to hold it down. I could not sleep, I sat in my chair and dozed, fearful of any noise, any movement.

A loud shaking rattle woke me with a start, my heart hammering furiously and it took several fearful moments before I realized that it was the compressor on my second-hand fridge banging and clattering as it sometimes did.

Next morning the last thing I felt like doing was going to work but I had no option.

When I got home that evening, my heart froze in hideous shock. Books were flung about in all directions, broken-spined and pages ripped. And the box was open!

I quickly drove down to B&Q and bought the heaviest, stickiest tape I could find and a ball of thick green nylon rope.

I taped down the lid, then wrapped tape round and round the box and finally tied it with the rope, using matches to fuse the ends of the rope together. Tomorrow I would take it down to the refuse dump.

Greatly fearful, I went to bed, almost too scared to sleep but I eventually did drop off. It was the cold that woke me and then my breath stopped, I felt as though I was suffocating, unable to drag air into my lungs, the sense of a malign presence overpowering. I threw myself off the bed and ran out into the lounge.

The tape around the box was sliced open as though by a razor, the rope was cleanly cut, and the box lid was open.

I did not dare sleep and as soon as B&Q was open, I bought glue, hammer and nails, staple gun, and thick plastic sheeting. I glued and then nailed down the lid, taped it and then stapled layers of plastic sheeting all around the box, completely sealing it.

As soon as the 'Ming Dynasty,' my local Chinese takeaway, opened at twelve, I asked to speak to the owner, a middle-aged Chinaman whom everybody called Ray, although I doubt it was his real name.

I passed him the parchment, 'Please,' I begged, 'Can you translate, it's very important.'

He began to read, then his eyes flickered up to mine. 'Where did you find this?'

'In a shop, antique shop.'

Ray carried on reading, every so often looking up to give me quizzical looks. Finally, he said, 'This is a message from the Mandarin of Shanghai province to Prince Kang in the Imperial Palace in Peking. After greetings and humble salutations, he says he is pleased to send as tribute the head of Li Hsui-Cheng, a very important rebel Taiping general and warlord. Do you know about the Taiping Revolution?' Ray asked.

'Vaguely. A bloody peasant revolution in about 1850? A lunatic thought he was the son of God and almost overthrew the Manchu dynasty? I read about it in a Flashman book.'

'Just so, many millions, maybe sixty million people died.'

Ray continued reading. 'It says that Li Hsui-Cheng was put to death by … ling-chi… the Death of a Thousand.'

'The Death of a Thousand?'

'Yes, many, many cuts on the body with a razor, skinning, stripping of flesh, cutting off… appendages, a very horrible way to die and reserved for the most important prisoners. Then he was beheaded, and the head sent to Prince Kang in a box, this is the ultimate punishment. For Chinese people it is very important for a body to be buried whole. When somebody is beheaded, the family must bribe the executioner to buy back the body and head to bury together, otherwise his spirit cannot meet with his ancestors, the spirit can then become very angry.' Ray handed me back the parchment. 'You have the box?'

'No, just the paper,' I lied.

'OK. You want to order now?'

Declining (food was the last thing on my mind) I hurried back home, dreading what I might find, but the head-box was as I had left it.

Remembering what Ray had said, I felt it important to try and return the box (and head) to China, Li Hsui-Cheng might find his ancestors more easily there.

I logged onto the internet and downloaded a Shanghai business directory. At random I chose the 'Golden Chrysanthemum Trading Company.' I then wrapped the box in brown paper with lots of Sellotape and string, addressed it and called a courier company to collect it for delivery to Shanghai.

Relief is not just a word. Relief is an emotion so powerful it left me totally drained. Exhausted, I went to bed early that night.

Once again, the cold woke me, the hairs rising at the back of my neck and the intense feeling of suffocation and of a malignant phantom presence paralyzing me.

'No,' I shouted, I've sent you back to China,' The suffocation grew worse and then I realized, the ghost, spirit, phantom, whatever you call it, had been out of the box when I sealed it. Now he was roaming free, an angry spirit.

A very angry spirit.

I SEE DEAD PEOPLE

I saw Elvis Presley once.

Nothing unusual about that you might say, after all millions of people- especially in America- must have seen Elvis.

The difference is – I saw him after he died.

You see, I'm like that boy in the film 'The Sixth Sense,' I too see dead people.

And so, not more than six months ago I saw Elvis – large as life. Well, not quite large as life, but you know what I mean. Large as death. Although quite what he was doing in the small Yorkshire village of Upper Blaylock, I can't imagine. But there he was, standing by the corner of High Street and Rathbone Road, just outside Wilkins Bakery and Sandwich Shop. Perhaps he was looking for a peanut butter and jelly sandwich? People hurried past him, hurried through him, oblivious to the fact that the world's greatest superstar was in their midst.

Elvis was wearing one of those white satin jumpsuits he used to wear for Las Vegas concerts, all flared trousers, high collar and covered in rhinestones – a bit out of place for a damp February in Yorkshire. He saw me looking, pointed a finger as though firing a gun, wiggled his hips, and laughed, although not out loud. Then he just faded away into the rain-soaked brickwork.

My friend Missy –short for Melissa, who can also see dead people – says it must have been an Elvis impersonator I saw, but I know what I saw, and it was Elvis. Definitely. One day, when I pass on to the other side, I'll ask him what he was doing in Upper Blaylock. I doubt it was for the scenery – unless he has an abiding interest in grassed over slag heaps and abandoned mine machinery.

I haven't always had this gift for seeing dead people, if in fact it is a gift? I wonder sometimes. It was only after a car crash, five years ago that it began to happen. Perhaps the 'gift' had always been there, latent, and it had taken the crash and a nasty head injury to release that potential.

The first dead person I saw (apart from my grandmother in her coffin but that does not really count) was my best friend Bill Jenkins, who had died in the crash.

We'd been to a football match over at High Yaxby, a village across the valley, followed by a meal and drink at the 'Black Bull.'

Bill was driving. I asked how many pints he'd drunk, and he swore he had only had a couple. He was telling the truth. He had only had a couple of pints but what he did not tell me was that he had had three or four vodka chasers as well. I sat in front with Bill while my wife, Jane, and Bill's girlfriend, Sue, sat in the back.

The weather had turned foul, heavy black clouds scudding across the glowering hills, rain squalls lashing across the twisting road down Harkside Edge. Bill lost it on the sharpest corner. Going far too fast in the foul conditions, he hit the rock wall to our left, bounced across the road, and straight through, almost straight over – the Armco barrier. How far we fell, somersaulting and tumbling, I can't tell. The girls were screaming, screeching metal, crashing echoes as we smashed into rocks, plummeting to the valley a hundred of feet below. Then black descending silence.

Bill was killed, so was Jane. Sue, well she remains in a vegetative state, unlikely ever to recover, her parents unable to take that irrevocable decision to turn of the machine, the only thing keeping their only child alive.

As for me, I lay in a coma for twenty-four days. And when I came to, I could see dead people.

Bill came to me first, carrying his left arm, torn off in the crash. He carried it like a club and swung it at my head in a mock attack. Sorry, I seemed to hear him although no sound escaped his bloodied lips. Sorry.

I saw him several times after that, and other dead people. Mr Patel, who lived in the next street and hanged himself one Sunday morning. Mrs Arble, Jennifer Mills who was knocked down on Seymour Street by a hit and run. And of course, Elvis. But as dearly as I wished, I never did see Jane, my lovely wife.

CABIN C69

The cruise liner *Anconia* eased up to its berth alongside the dock at Port Royal, Trinidad, as out on the dockside a colourful steel band played a welcoming calypso.

Anconia was on the return leg of a cruise through the Caribbean and up the Amazon River, when, off the coast of Guyana, she was hit by an unexpectedly severe storm. Although little damage was done to the ship apart from some broken crockery and glassware, several of the crew and passengers on board received minor injuries whilst an elderly lady broke her hip and arm in a fall It was not however, the only incident on that fateful voyage.

After *Anconia* had tied up, a junior officer reported to the bridge, 'Captain, the police are here.'

Two years later.

My wife and I were on a Baltic cruise when, over dinner, we got talking to Martin and Laura Kendrick from Leeds. Afterwards we went for a drink where they told us this remarkable tale.

Last February, Laura said, they had been on board the *Anconia* cruising the Caribbean and up the Amazon, then back to Barbados via Trinidad and St. Vincent.

They were sailing northwards from the Amazon towards Trinidad and after a nightcap in the bar, went down to their cabin, cabin C69.

'When we are at sea, we never fully close the curtains, nobody can see in and we like to see the sunrise come in through the glazed balcony door,' said Laura.

What it was that woke her that night, she couldn't say. It felt chilly, almost icy, and a sense of almost palpable dread surged over her. Beside her, Martin snored heavily, as he always did after a few drinks. Her heart pounded fiercely and for a minute or two she thought she was having a heart attack. She nudged Martin to wake him, but he was unresponsive except to roll over and start to snore again.

'Martin, wake up, wake up, 'she said, shaking him vigorously, and gradually he came round. 'What? What's up?'

'I don't feel right, funny, cold and fearful. I've had palpitations.'

'Probably those prawns you ate, I told you they looked dodgy.'

'It's not the prawns, I tell you. Something is not right. Not right.'

'Like what?'

'If I knew, you idiot, I wouldn't feel like this, would I?'

'No, s'pose not,' Martin answered reluctantly before closing his eyes to go back to sleep. 'Take one of your seasick pills, that'll make you feel better.'

'It's not seasickness, Martin. There is something

wrong I tell you. Can't you feel the cold? We're almost at the Equator, it shouldn't be cold like this.'

'Turn the air-conditioning down then.'

'It's not even on.'

'Oh! Don't know then.'

'I'm worried, really worried, I know that there's something wrong. Not right.'

'Woman's intuition, is it?'

'I could have hit him' Laura told us.

She got out of bed to go to the toilet as Martin reluctantly sat up and turned on the bedside lamp, then picked up his book and began to read.

'I had a wash to wake myself and find out what was wrong,' Laura said, 'and I then looked out towards the balcony. And screamed.'

There was a man on the balcony, staring in, wild-eyed and frantic, his hands scrabbling at the glass, as if scratching at it. 'I only had a thin shortie nightie on, and you could see everything there is to see. I screamed again. 'There's a man on the balcony. A Man! Staring in! Martin!

'You just carried on reading, didn't you Martin, and said something about not being ridiculous, how could there be anybody out there, we're in the middle of the ocean. Tried to make out it was my reflection I could see, well, I know what a man looks like and it was a man.'

'Get up' I screamed, 'do something for God's sake, do something!'

'I jumped out of bed then,' Martin interjected, 'Even though I was stark naked.' At which Laura rolled her eyes, as if to say, how is that in any way relevant. 'And yeah, there was something or somebody there. I ran over to the door, Laura screaming, 'Don't open the door, don't open the door.' As if I was going to. I yelled at him through the glass. 'Go on, go away. Get out,' pointing to the right, thinking he'd come from the cabin next door, we'd seen him peering through the gaps in the dividing screen when Laura was in her swimming costume, weirdo, we'd said to each other. You get them sometimes, weirdos, don't you?'

'Get on with it, Martin!' Laura snapped.

'I banged on the glass, hard, but he didn't seem to hear me. I yelled at him to eff off, but he just stared, stared, and stared. And was scary, really scary, I don't mind telling you. And felt it too, the cold and the evil in him. He had wild, bloodshot eyes, and there were scratches down his face, three or four long raking scratches as if he'd been fighting a cat.'

'Or his wife'

'You see, we both still thought it was the weirdo next door, that he'd somehow climbed over or around the screen. I yelled at Laura to call security, what's the number she shouted, I don't know, call anybody, reception, room service, anybody, just get somebody in here.'

'I called reception and said there was an intruder on the balcony, but they didn't believe me at first, said I must be imagining it, giving the impression I'd had too much to drink, but eventually I persuaded them to come and check,' Laura said as Martin carried on talking, gesticulating wildly as he spoke.

'He was like a madman, he suddenly started screaming and screaming, but you couldn't hear anything, his face contorted and twisted. You could feel the anger and hate and evil, pure evil just pouring out of him. Laura had called reception or whoever and there was a knocking at the door.'

'I'd wrapped a towel around myself by then,' continued Laura, 'and they came in, security or whatever, or two or three of them. They went straight over to the balcony. You could see something was still there. They opened the door and he just vanished. Vanished, like that! But there was a terrible icy wind which blew through the cabin.'

'It was more like Arctic sea spray,' contradicted Martin, 'I was closest and felt it most.'

'It's not a competition, Martin,' Laura snapped.

'Whatever, you could see from the guys faces, the security guys, that they didn't really believe us, no matter how much we insisted somebody had been out there. We couldn't go back to sleep after they left, too scared, so we just sat on the bed, waiting for morning.'

'The next afternoon we got a request from the captain to meet and discuss what had happened,' Laura said. 'We thought we would be reprimanded, or even put off the ship for creating a false alarm but he was dead nice about it, the captain, wasn't he, Martin?'

'Yes, he told us…'

'Let me, you'll only get it wrong, back to front.'

'OK,' Martin answered reluctantly.

'He said, the captain, that two years ago, they had had a man overboard incident, that's what he called it. A man overboard incident.'

'Yes, just about where we were last night and…'

'Martin! Yes, just about where we were last night. It seems that Andrew Slater and his wife, Shirley, were in cabin C69.'

'Same as ours.'

'Yes! All voyage they had been rowing and arguing, everybody on the ship heard them.'

'And they drank heavily.'

'Yes, Martin! They drank heavily, and the night of the... incident Andrew Salter got very drunk, really loud, and aggressive, shouting and swearing at Shirley. He had to be warned about his behaviour, there had been complaints from other passengers, warned if he did not behave, they would be put off the ship at the next port.'

'Trinidad.'

'Martin. Am I telling this or you? They went back to C69, and apparently there was a quite nasty storm that night, the captain said, and about 2 a.m. Shirley rang reception, in a panic, saying that Andrew had tried to kill her, to throw her overboard but had gone over himself instead.

'Fallen over the balcony.'

'Obviously! He had dragged her out onto the balcony by her hair and stood on the little drinks table to get more leverage to tip her over when the ship lurched in the storm and being so pissed, he had overbalanced and went over himself. Leastwise that was her story and she had black eye and other bruises to corroborate it. They turned the ship around to search for him but, they couldn't find him.'

'The police in Trinidad interviewed her, Shirley, and the couples in the next cabins, they'd heard all the shouting and screaming but had seen nothing. They let her go, they had to.'

'And she was interviewed by the police in England when she got back, of course.'

'And there was an inquest.'

'Yes, thank you, Martin. Yes, open verdict, the coroner ruled, no evidence either way, but... according to the captain, Andrew Slater's first wife had died in mysterious circumstances and there had also been domestic violence, but it never got to court.'

'So, it makes you think, doesn't it?

'Yes, Martin, it does! Then I said to the captain, what are you telling us, that it was Andrew Slater's ghost we saw last night. No, no, not at all, he said, I am simply giving you some information which could be relevant to what happened to you last night. So, you can come to your own conclusions. Then we asked if we could move cabins? We didn't want to go back in C69 but there was nothing else available.

''It was awful, there was still that cold, creepy atmosphere, really creepy.'

'So, whatever you do, if you ever go on the *Anconia*, don't take cabin C69!'

My wife and I looked at each other. We had just booked a Mediterranean cruise on *Anconia*. And had been allocated cabin C69.

ANGEL

She smelled like angels ought to smell. That's a line from a film I once saw.

She smelled like an angel and looked like an angel. Only without the wings! Tall, leggy, blonde, a figure to die for! Or to kill for! All of it expensively dressed in a cream silk suit that probably cost more than I earn in a year. Correction – make that five years plus an arm and leg and other assorted appendages.

Her perfume, subtle and sexy, wafted over me like a caress.

'I want you to find my husband,' she said.

'I want to kiss your feet,' I answered. Actually, no I didn't, but I thought it.

'Tell me,' I answered. Just to put you in the picture, I'm a private investigator. A not very successful private investigator, not Magnum PI, Mullins PI.

Her name was Angela Mackenzie and she told me that her husband, Gregory Mackenzie, local businessman, owner of a chain of regional newspapers, seriously rich, had gone missing, been missing for three days without trace. The police were not interested, she said, and now she, his second wife, wanted me to find him. For me, he could stay missing for as long as he liked. Forever in fact.

She gave me his photo, a tall powerful-looking man in his late fifties, confident and sure of himself. Seriously wealthy, just the sort of man to entice a woman like Angela the Angel. I hated him.

We agreed on my fees, a daily rate plus expenses. This is not a public enquiry. Private Investigation.

She walked away, taking a piece, a very large piece, of my heart with her. Stop making a fool of yourself, I scolded, but I didn't listen. I never do.

Two days later she came back, asking for a report. She still smelled like angels ought to smell. I reported. Sorry, no progress but would keep trying.

'Thank you, I know you won't let me down.' She leaned over and kissed me on the cheek. And walked away, taking the rest of my heart with her.

I scolded myself again. But to no avail.

I tried to find him. I really did. Honest. But I could find no trace. He did not use his credit cards, at least not in this country, had left his BMW at his house, took no clothes, had not withdrawn large amounts of cash from his account, had no enemies as far as I could see. No known mistresses. No known vices.

Angel came again to see me for a report on progress. Or lack of progress.

She came back again three days later. He's come back she said, and I hated him even more. He went to Spain on business, a last-minute thing, serious negotiations to buy an English language newspaper to cater for the expatriate British living in Spain. He's done it before, several times in fact, going off without telling her but usually calls in a after a day or so. Then she asked me take coffee with her. I said yes. If she had asked me to take arsenic, my answer would have been the same. We took coffee in the lounge of the 'Black Bull Hotel.'

'I hate him,' she said, staring into the bottom of her coffee cup.

'Why did you ask me to look for him, then?' I asked.

'So I could kill him!'

I should have been surprised but somehow, I wasn't.

'I hate him,' she said again. 'He makes my life a living hell.'

I hated him too.

Once she had started talking, there was no stopping.

'We have a daughter, Melody.'

'Lovely name,' I said stupidly, 'very musical.' She ignored me, but that's OK, I'm used to beautiful angels ignoring me.

'She's thirteen, just developing, you understand. She is such a pretty girl. And he looks at her. Looks at her that way, you know, and I am afraid for her.' She stared at me intently, a soft tear, like a brilliant pearl, starting from the corner of her cornflower blue eyes. I wanted to kiss that tear and take away the salt of her pain. 'I was an abused child myself. My father, from the age of twelve, he… abused me… that way. I know the damage it does, and I cannot bear for it to happen to Melody.'

'Why don't you just leave him?'

'I cannot. You don't know him. He is evil. Pure evil. He would destroy me. And Melody. I could not bear it if he harmed Melody.'

'Then go to the police, they should be involved if there is a suggestion of child abuse.'

'There is nothing they could do because he would destroy her mentally.'

She wiped away her tear. 'You see, he, Gregory, keeps a file on me. When I was young, still a teenager– I had another daughter – Samantha. I was a single mother – no job. No prospects. No money. So, I did what I had to do to survive. You know, I did what a girl has to do to survive. You don't need me to draw you a picture.' No but a photograph would be OK. 'There were arrests. Prosecutions. Social Services were involved, and they took Samantha away from me. He has copies of all the records, and he will use them against me, and he would make a case for me not being a fit mother.'

She reached over and took my hand in hers. 'You understand, if I stay, I know he will abuse Melody. And if I leave, he will publish the file in his newspapers and use that information to get custody of Melody. And how could I live with myself knowing that Melody knows what her mother had been? And how can I live if I let him abuse her? As I know he will.'

She didn't need to ask me. I knew what had to be done. A man who had gone missing without trace for ten days can go missing forever.

I nodded, not saying a word.

'Thank you, she whispered and stood up, my hand still in hers. 'Take a room here. Help me forget for a while.' My heart seized solid, and I suddenly found it hard to breathe. 'Go up first and I'll follow, I don't want to be seen.'

I booked the room, and we went upstairs. You don't need to know the details.

'I love you,' she said as she left. 'Very much, but... we can't be together whilst ever...'

The next day I began to plan the murder of Gregory Mackenzie, latent child abuser and tormentor of my angel.

Killing a man is easy when you have the right motivation. I simply waited by the side of his house, hidden in the shadows. He drove up, used a remote to open the garage door, and as he got out of the car I ran inside the garage and garrotted him. Easy.

The hard part was the disposal of the body. Burial? Bodies can be found, sniffer dogs and all that. Burning, terrible smell and the neighbours complain. Concrete boots and a one-way trip out to sea would be the best solution. Except I don't have a boat and the cross-channel ferry might object if I started dropping corpses over the stern rail. Apart from that I get seasick. So, I drove up to Norfolk, hired a small motorboat on the Broads and in the dark of the night carried Gregory Mackenzie's body aboard. Tied a couple of concrete blocks I stole from a building site to his feet and round his neck, drove out to a quiet backwater and tipped him over. With barely a splash he sank below the brownish waters.

When I returned home, the police were waiting, and arrested me on suspicion of murder.

A strange man had been reported acting suspiciously – a nosey neighbour no doubt, you can't go about killing anybody these days without some lace-curtained busybody interfering.

Forensic science placed me in the garage, there were smears of his blood where he had fallen against the garage wall, specks of his blood on my shoes and there was a description of my car. The boat owner confirmed the hire, further forensics (blood traces and hairs from his head) proved that Gregory had been in the boot of my car and on the boat and police frogmen quickly found his body. I was charged with murder.

I could have told the police everything then, about Melody and the threats that Gregory Mackenzie posed but that could have been just as damaging to Melody as if he had published the details of Angela's past in his sordid newspapers. I said nothing, I knew that if things went wrong at the trial, I could rely on Angela to come and give evidence in my defence – I knew I would still be guilty of killing Mackenzie but would possibly get a light sentence and be free in four or five years. And Angel would be waiting – I knew she would.

How wrong can you be?

Principal witness for the prosecution – Angela Mackenzie, tearfully giving her evidence against me, damning me to the jury, 'Yes your Honour, the man in the dock was the man I saw lurking by my house, just before my dear husband arrived home and was so cruelly taken away from me.'

I called an urgent consultation with my defence lawyers - told them everything. The threat to Melody, Angela's secret past and the blackmail files. The reason behind the killing. They brought in the investigating Police officers.

The next day they were back, and my world fell apart. The Mackenzie's had no children. There was no Melody, unchained or otherwise. There were no past convictions against Angela, no hidden secrets at all.

I got life, to serve a minimum of nineteen years before possibility of parole.

Angela came to see me in my cell before I was

taken away to serve my sentence. 'Pathetic fool' she whispered and walked away. Not Magnum PI, Muggins PI!

She still smelled like an angel ought to smell.

The Angel of Death.

WHAT I DID ON MY SUMMER HOLIDAYS

Mum and Dad decided on a boring farm holiday this summer.

I wanted us to go somewhere else, anywhere else, except to a mouldy farm looking at cows, sheep, and tractors all day long.

'But there'll be lots to do,' said Mum, 'look, here's the brochure, you can go pony trekking, hire a trail bike, there's lovely walks across the moors and it's not too far down to the coast. You'll just love it, David. I know you will if you'll only just give it a chance.'

'It sounds dead boring to me.'

'At least give it a try.'

'Why can't we go to Florida, to Disneyworld, much better than some boring old farm?'

'Well, we can't really afford it this year, maybe next year, eh?'

'That's what you said last year.'

'I know, but things have been a bit difficult this year for Dad at work and with one thing and another, we just don't have the money.'

'Why don't we stay at home then, at least I've got my friends here?'

'Your dad needs a break. We all need a break. Look, it's a lovely farmhouse, right up on the moors with beautiful views. It's a proper working farm and we'll be staying in these cottages next to the farmhouse, it'll be something special we've never done before.'

'And'll never do again because we'll have all have died from boredom.'

'Don't be negative, David, think of it as an experience.'

Well, it was certainly that.

The farm was actually quite pretty; the main house was white-painted with red tile roofs and tall chimneys built around a courtyard. Our accommodation was a cottage across the other side of the courtyard and to be fair it was very nice with two small bedrooms upstairs, a bathroom, living room, and small kitchen in case we had wanted to self-cater, but Mum said she was on holiday as well and she wasn't going to spend her vacation cooking for everybody else.

The garden was set out with tables and chairs where we could sit out and look out across the fields to the moors beyond. At the bottom of the lower fields there was a large wood, full of pigeons and squabbling rooks and a big pond beneath the trees with ducks and geese and Mrs. Salmon, the farmer's wife, said if I was very quiet, I might get to see a kingfisher, but I never did.

For the first two days I sat and sulked, sitting with my back to the views and determined to hate every minute of every day.

But then I began to explore, the working farm was OK, but once you've seen one tractor or one black and white cow you've seen them all, but I did get to enjoy going off into the moors by myself. Sometimes I hired a trail bike, and Mum and Dad were happy enough to let me go out on my own.

I went pony trekking once, but that was boring, just sitting on the pony as the riding instructor led me along, it might have been alright if I could have gone off on my own and galloped across the moors but as it was, we barely got into a fast walk, let alone a gallop.

I also enjoyed going down to the wood at the bottom of the fields, although as I say, I never did get to see that kingfisher. One of the big trees had heavy branches jutting out right across the pond. You could tell that there had once been a swing tied to one of the branches, there was a deep cut groove where the rope had been and on both banks the ground was deeply worn away where swing-users ran to grab the rope and where they had landed the other side.

It was by the pond that I first saw Eric.

He was on the other side, standing in shadow, looking at me. He was about my age, dressed in grey shorts, and a grey short-sleeved shirt.

We stood looking at each other for a while, saying not a word.

'Hello,' I said at last. 'Do you live round here, then?' He was obviously not a holiday maker.

He nodded slowly in assent but still said nothing. Country bumpkin I thought cruelly, wondering if he was perhaps a bit slow-witted, inbred, and retarded. Maybe he came from a family of axe-murdering cannibals.

'Hi, I'm David. I'm here on holiday, staying up at the farmhouse.'

'I know,' he answered, his voice barely carrying across the water. 'I'm Eric. I live here.'

'On the farm?'

He nodded again and then turned and ran away, disappearing into the deep shadows of the wood so quickly I couldn't even see in which direction he went.

'Be like that, then,' I said to his departing back, but I doubt he heard me.

I mooched back to the farm, bored and listless, kicking at things, disquieted for reasons I could not explain.

The pebbles rattling against the bedroom window startled me, I had been dozing in an edgy half-sleep and the clicking sound of the stones shot through me like gunshots. Jerking fully awake, I went over to the window and looked out. Eric stood below, bathed in moonlight, an eerie spectral glow about his upturned face. He saw me looking and beckoned me to come down. I checked the time. Just gone midnight. Mum and Dad were in bed asleep, in fact I could hear Dad snoring through the cottage walls.

Another impatient rattle of pebbles against the glass.

I quickly dressed, pulling my Bart Simpson sweatshirt on over my T-shirt as it was sure to be cold out and carrying my trainers in my hand, I crept down the stairs, the creaking of the ancient timbers under my feet echoing loudly in my ears, sure that the noise would wake the dead, let alone Mum and Dad.

Eric was waiting by the front door. He put a finger to his mouth to tell me to keep quiet and then hurried away, careful to avoid the gravel driveway. We ran across the fields as moonlight flickered through scudding clouds.

'Where are we going? I asked when we were clear of the house, but he said nothing, just carried on leading me across the fields until we came to a small copse.

He waved his hand, palm downwards to tell me to slow down and held his finger to his mouth again.

Slowly we crept forward and then got down on our bellies and slid until we came to the lip of a shallow depression and quietly, cautiously we peered over. On the far side of the depression, which was shaped like a giant cereal bowl set into the ground, a pair of badgers watched whilst three young badgers, cubs or kits or whatever young badgers are called romped and rolled and play-fought, bathed in the silvery sheen of moonlight.

It was magical, absolutely brilliant, one of the best, most exciting things I have ever witnessed in my entire life. I don't know how long we watched them but suddenly one the badgers cocked his ears, barked a warning and in a flash all five badgers scampered across the bowl and disappeared into their sett.

I checked my watch – 2:30 – 'I'd better get back,' I whispered. 'See you tomorrow by the pond, OK?' Eric said nothing as usual but just nodded. I got up and hurried back to the farm, worried by now that my absence would have been discovered, but no, they were still snoring away when I crept back upstairs again.

When I got to the pond next morning, there was no sign of Eric, but a rope hung from the overhanging bough with several big knots at the bottom end of the rope to stop your hands sliding down. Then Eric appeared on the other side, he ran, leapt, grabbed hold of the rope, and swung across like Tarzan, letting go at the end of his trajectory to land lightly beside me. He gestured for me to have a go and I did, it was good fun.

. . .

We'd each had a dozen or so swings before Eric suddenly let go halfway across and holding his knees landed in the pond in a great bombshell scattering the ducks and geese in panic.

He waved for me to do the same. I didn't want to get all my clothes wet so I took off my trainers and socks and T-shirt and in just my shorts, did the same.

SPLASH.

I surfaced, looking for Eric but he was not to be seen. Then one of my ankles was seized and I was dragged under again, gulping in foul-tasting pond water as I struggled to get to the surface, but Eric clung tight. Beyond a joke, Eric, I thought as I fought to surface, desperate for air, my head swimming. He was clinging higher up my legs now, and then he had me by the waist, his legs clamped tightly round mine. His spectral face came into view and I heard him – heard him – saying. Lonely, lonely, stay with me, stay with me, David. Stay forever.

The more I struggled to rise, the tighter he clung, and I knew that I was drowning, scarlet flashes bursting in my brain like lightning bolts.

I forced myself to sink and then as my feet hit bottom I dipped even further, bending my knees and then with all the explosive effort I could muster I thrust myself to the surface and out of Eric's grasp. I gulped air and then swam as fast as I could. I felt him grasping at my ankles again, but I broke free, reached the bank, and scrambled out, fleeing for all I was worth back to the farm, leaving my clothes behind.

I never went back. All night I lay awake, every night I lay awake, dreading the sound of pebbles against the window or expecting Eric's spectral form to ooze through the walls and seize me again.

It was only as we were leaving, I had the courage to ask the farmer's wife if there was a boy called Eric on the farm.

'Oh no, David, dear, no Eric here now, although there was an Eric, son of one of our cowmen. Jack Pope's boy, about your age 'e was but he drowned in that pond, ooh, now, must be all of ten year since. Terrible tragedy it was...

The room swam and I could hear Eric's voice again. Lonely, lonely, stay with me, David. Stay with me FOREVERRRRR...

I ran to the car, climbed in, and locked the doors behind me, fearfully expecting his silver-skinned face to appear at the window, fearful that he might somehow get into the car, or follow it and that one night, at home in my bed, I would hear the rattle of pebbles against my window.

NOT MUCH OF A FUNERAL

After my father's funeral I went round to the empty house to put his affairs in order and sort out the paperwork. In his desk, amongst the Title Deeds, insurance policies, copies of bank statements etc, I found this document, written by his grandfather, my great-grandfather, Willard James Halcrow. He must have written it shortly after his return from Gallipoli in 1915.

He had written:

It was not much a funeral, considering he was an Officer and a Gentleman, but I suppose we were in the middle of a battle against the Turks at the time.

The assault on the Turkish positions had been a failure, just like every other action in that ill-conceived Gallipoli campaign We had attacked in the late morning, charging uphill through the scrub, the Turks well entrenched on the hilltops above us, pouring down lethal fire into our massed ranks as we struggled up the steep slopes.

I hardly got to fire a shot as the battalion was decimated alongside me, all my mates dead or severely wounded. We had joined up all together in October 1914: the apprentices, lathe operators, packers, and gaffers from the Alexander & Matthews Metalworks Company.

Two days earlier we had disembarked at Sulva Bay and then were sent up the slopes to capture this hill. I could not even tell you what the hill was called, they all looked alike to me, steeply sloped, sliced across with deep ravines, all but barren of vegetation apart from scrub and bushes and the occasional pine tree, inhospitable land and if you want my opinion, the Turks were welcome to it.

Despite our losses, we struggled on. All was confusion and noise and dust, screaming shells, heat, machine gun bullets, sniper fire, the shouts and screams of the wounded, blasts on whistles as helpless subalterns tried to keep the handful of surviving troops together and advancing on up the bitter slopes.

It was somewhere about then that the company captain, Captain the Honourable Gerard Barclay-Milnes was mortally wounded, I did not see him fall but with him down, the attack, what was left of it, faltered. The remnants of the battalion took what cover we could and waited out for the night and relief.

When the deep velvet night had settled over the battleground the stretcher bearers came and took what wounded they could, and our shattered battalion retreated back down the slopes.

Captain Barclay-Milnes died of his wounds that night.

His funeral was held the following morning. The assembled battalion, such as was left, were drawn up in ranks about the grave as Captain Barclay-Milnes was buried. A chaplain read the lesson and eulogy and a bugler sounded the Last Post and the funeral was over.

As I say, it was not much of a funeral.

The captain was the son of Lord Exham, a local land and mine owner, and his father had used his influence to fix a commission for him.

After four day's rest, we were sent back up to the hills, to another hill taken by the Lancashire's a week or so ago.

All I remember of that time was the heat, the flies, and the all-pervading stink of the rotting dead, British, Turk, out there beyond the trench line in No-Man's-Land.

It was about the fourth day of our stint. Edgar Garforth was in the trench beside me. I took out my cigarettes and offered him one, and we lit up and leaned back against the trench wall, trying to find a little shade from the furnace-hammer heat of the Gallipoli sun. Flies swarmed thickly about us, crawling into our ears and eyes and nostrils, attracted by our sweat, undeterred by the tobacco smoke. *What a hateful land, who would want to be buried in this godforsaken country,* I thought, remembering the captain.

'Shame about Captain Barclay-Milnes,' I said, by way of making conversation.

'Aye? Is it?' he replied. 'Not to me it isn't, not by a long chalk.'

'Lord Exham'll be right cut up, losing his only son and heir like that.'

'I'll lose no sleep over that.'

'Aye? He seemed a decent enough bloke to me, for an officer, that is.'

'Is that so? Not from where I'm sittin' he weren't.'

'What did he do to you then, put you on report or summat?'

'I'll tell thee a story,' he said, stubbing out his fag and getting out his own crumpled packet of Gold Flake, passing one to me. 'A true story about the Honourable Gerard Barclay-Milnes'

'You knew him from afore, like?'

'Well, you couldn't say we moved in the same social circles, but aye, I knew him alright, knew him for what he was.'

Edgar paused, marshalling his thoughts as he fixed his gaze on the sun-dried, rat-chewed hand of a dead Turk clutching at a strand of tangled barbed wire just beyond the lip of the parapet, 'Uncle Abdul' we called the dead Turk, don't ask me why but every new platoon occupying the trench was introduced to him that way. 'Say hello to Uncle Abdul' the departing troops would say to the newcomers.

'My father,' Edgar said at last, 'he's a labourer on one of Lord Exham's farms, up the valley in West Haddon. We've got a tied cottage, goes with the job, like. It's only a small place: front room; kitchen; and two bedrooms; one for me Dad and Mam and the wee bairns, one for the bigger kids, all four on us. It got to be a might crowded, especially when we got a bit older, me and big brother Billy and two grown sisters all in the same bed, like, topped and toed, them at top and us at bottom.'

I said nothing, just let Edgar talk.

'Eleanor, she were sixteen, going on seventeen. Always a dreamer she was, head in the clouds. Pretty as a picture. Loved animals, she did, not just them on't farm but the wild ones an'all. She knew where there were badger setts and fox burrows and spent hours watching them. She could spend a day just watching the clouds float by could our Eleanor. She were… gentle and trusting, not really of this world if you know what I mean?'

'Aye.'

'One day, just before war broke out, she were in this secret place she had, sort of a hollow by the river. She hears shouting and sounds of a horse neighing and so she goes to look. Sees Gerard Barclay-Milnes beating his horse. Seemed like the beast had gone lame and the Honourable Gerard were hacked off about it, slashing at the poor beast with his whip. Eleanor, she can't stand to see cruelty to animals, makes her physically sick, it does.

'She… what's the word? She… remonstrates wi' him. What's it to do with you? he says, 'cos he don't like being crossed. He can see she's a labourer's lass right enough, what with her hand-me-down patched dresses, always clean as a new pin mind, but obvious she's dead poor and there's nobody poorer than a farm labourer. Says she's trespassing on his lands and in big trouble. She'll go to jail, stuff like that. Scares her summat wicked, Then, he rapes her. Just like that, knocks her to the ground, drags up her clothes and rapes her. Not once but twice.'

'Jesus wept.'

'Aye, it's enough to make a man blaspheme and worse. Then he threatens if she tells it'll be the worst for her. Nobody'll believe her over him and he'll make sure we was tossed out of our home and our Mam sent to the poorhouse. You can imagine what a state that put her in.'

'The bastard.'

'Took me Mam days to get the story out on her. Terrified she was and full of shame, blaming herself, fearful we was going to lose our home on her account. Eventually though Mam did get it out of her. My Dad was all for going after him wi' a shotgun but what good would that have done? There was nowt we could do. Police? What're they goin' to do, our Eleanor's word against that of a lord's son?'

'Aye well, I can see why you're not right upset at his death, then.'

"That's not the whole of it. On the attack the other day, I were out to the left flank and I sees Barclay-Milnes up ahead of me, fifty-sixty yards or so. So, I shot him. Right in the middle of his back. There was so many bullets flying about, one more made no difference. So there we 'as it, it was me as shot him and I'm right glad about it.'

'Why've you told me? Aren't you worried in case I blab?'

'Had to tell someone, didn't I? And anyhow, my word agin yours. Nobody'll prove a thing.'

'Don't worry, I'm saying nowt, the bastard got what he deserved, you ask me.'

'Aye, that's my way of thinking an' all.'

"What about Eleanor, you going to tell her, tell her you've avenged her honour, like?"

'Eleanor? Aye, well the thing is, two weeks after, she went back to her secret place and hanged herself. Hanged herself from shame.

To this day I've never divulged what Edgar Garforth told me to another soul.

He died himself later on from dysentery.

This is a true statement.

. . .

Signed by my great-grandfather, Willard James Halcrow.

After a while, pondering what to do, I went into the kitchen and burned Great-grandfather's statement in the kitchen sink. Too much time has passed since then.

What good would it do to resurrect so many distant ghosts?

DEATH PALE WERE THEY ALL

Ambrose Curtain grimaced as he finished off his muesli, his mouth feeling gritty and sticky at the same time. Muesli with skimmed milk! He didn't really like the stuff but he had read somewhere that it is supposed to be good for you. He carefully wiped his mouth on his napkin and then opened up his post, gutting the envelopes with a brass paperknife that his Aunt Jean had brought back from Malta.

'*Dear Sir,* he read, *'unless funds are made immediately available to cover the cheque that has been returned by your bank...*

Ambrose sighed, these days his post seemed to consist solely of dunning letters, that and offers to subscribe to magazines in which he had absolutely no interest. – 'Ferret Fanciers Weekly' or 'Macramé for Men'. *If only I had got the chief accountant's job,* he told himself. *Everything would have been all right then, money wise. The job should have been be mine by rights anyway. After all, I've been working in the Finance Department at Silver's for years, a lot longer than Ingrid Dobson, that's for sure. And who was it that upgraded the computer systems and installed all the new accounting programs, and all that unpaid overtime? Me! But who did they give the job to, Ingrid bloody Dobson, that's who, just to prove that they are PC and don't discriminate against women? Equal rights and all that bollocks. Well, what about my rights, eh?*

He looked at the collection agency's letter again. What was particularly galling was not the threat of legal action and unspecified mayhem to be inflicted on his person but the fact that the letter was not even addressed to him by name. *It's as though I don't even exist as a person in my own right, as if I'm only a 'Dear sir', unless...*

Ambrose poured himself another cup of tea and added a drop or two of skimmed milk; it looked (and tasted) like watered down white emulsion paint but it was supposed to better for you than full-fat milk. He then washed and dried his cup and cereal bowl and put them away in the cupboard and checked to make sure he had put the milk back in the fridge.

He went to the bathroom down the corridor from his rented bedsit, used the toilet, and then afterwards carefully washed his hands. He straightened his tie in front of the washbowl mirror, grimacing at his pallid, acne-scarred, thin faced reflection. *What I'd like out of life, is once, just for once, for my name to be in the newspapers,* Ambrose thought to himself, *for my name to be in the papers and to be made up to chief accountant, that's all. I reckon I could sell my soul for that. Not too much to ask, is it?*

He sighed deeply at the iniquities of an unfair world, that unfair world which had given Ingrid Dobson *his* job, just because she was a woman and probably a lesbian to boot.

Back in his room he put on his jacket and, even though it was forecast fine, carried his overcoat as well. Carefully locking his door behind him, his landlady was too nosey by half, he set off for work, still seething with suppressed indignation. Had there been a cat nearby he would have kicked it.

The weather had turned by the time he got home again. Black clouds scudded across a dirty grey sky and large drops of rain began to fall as he fumbled to get his key into the front door lock. As he opened the door a young man scurried over from a car parked nearby. 'Mr Curtain?' he asked, 'Mr Curtain?' Ambrose, fearing that the man was another debt collector, tried to close the door, but was too late. The young man stuck a polished shoe into the jamb and put his shoulder to the door, forcing Ambrose back into the hallway.

'Sorry 'bout barging in like this but it's going to be cats and dogs out there in a minute and I don't want my new suit getting wet, now do I?'

A door at the end of the hall opened and a suspicious prune of a face peered out.

'Iz that you Mr Curtain? And you haf visitor?'

'Yes Mrs Kubic.'

'You know ze rules, no girls in room.'

'S'alright Mrs. Kubic,' called out the young man. 'I'm no girl, leastwise not last time I looked.'

'Don't want filthy perverts either, leaving AIDS on toilet seat.'

'Only aids I've got are hearing aids!' He nudged Ambrose with his elbow. 'Know how you get hearing AIDS? No? From listening to arseholes! He laughed delightedly at his own joke, repeated the punch line, and then put his hand on Ambrose's shoulder. 'Now then Ambrose my little petal, how's about we go inside, out of sight of big flappin' ears? Eh?"

'Whatever you are selling, I don't want it. And if it's about that cheque?'

'It's not me what's selling, squire, it's you.'

'Me? I'm not selling anything, you must be mistaken.'

'That's not what you said this morning, now is it, sunshine?' the man said, taking Ambrose by his arm and leading him into his bedsit, standing at his elbow as Ambrose unlocked his door, giving him no room to escape or to dart into his room and shut the door.

Ambrose felt strange, as though things were beyond comprehension. He had never been skiing—far too dangerous, the cause of more fatal accidents than any other sport or so he had read—but he could imagine how it might feel to hurtle down a snowy slope out of control and that was exactly how he felt now.

There was only one easy chair in the sparsely furnished bedsit that Ambrose rented from Mrs Kubic, and the intrusive young man immediately took that and grandiosely waved Ambrose onto the bed. He then opened a thin brown briefcase and took out an imitation leather Filofax with 'Maid in Taiwam' stamped in gold letters on the back cover. Flipping it open, he handed Ambrose a business card which read: *M. Oxford. Salesman, MEPHISTO UNIVERSAL ENTERPRISES.* The company logo, a small red trident, was in the left-hand corner.

'Mephisto Enterprises?' Ambrose asked, fairly certain that he owed no money to a company by that name.

'That's right, old family business, been around for years and years.'

'What do you want with me? I'm not buying anything, encyclopaedias, anything like that.'

'Like I said, Ambrose, old son, it's you what's doing the selling. This morning you offered to sell your soul in exchange for two nights with Miss World, a red Porsche, and a ticket to Disneyworld. Oh no, sorry, that was the vicar! You want? Let me see?' he said, consulting his Filofax, 'oh yeah, now I got it, you want for your name to be in the papers and to get to be chief accountant where you work? Right?"

'Yes… but…' Ambrose felt totally disorientated, his brain like rice pudding, 'How?' He looked at the business card again, 'Mr. Oxford, how can you possibly know I said that?'

'Morris, call me Morris. As to 'ow we know, well, that's down to the boss, isn't' it? 'E knows everything 'bout everybody. 'Big D' we calls him, but not to his face, of course. We 'as to call him sir, but senior line managers and such, they get to call him Nick, Nick Mephisto. 'Old Nick' to you and me.'

'Mephisto! Old Nick! Oh my God, the devil!' exclaimed Ambrose, half-stifling an involuntary scream, an ice-water chill settling through his bones.

'Come on, Ambrose, don't take on so. It's only a straightforward business deal. It's what you want, in exchange for your soul. Which you don't use anyway'

Morris leaned forward earnestly in the chair. 'Look Ambrose, I know what you're thinking. You sell your soul and then it's off to Hell and Everlasting Fire and Brimstone, up to your armpits in imps and little demons sticking red-hot pitchforks up your bum all day. Right? Well, it's not like that at all. Honest, all that's just adverse propaganda put out by the other side. Listen you got a DVD player here? 'Cos I got a promo DVD here to show you what it's like. No? Well, you just take my word for it it's nothing like what it's made out to be by the competition. Course I ain't saying its Paradise, but then, what is these days?'

'Have? Have you...'

'What? Sold the soul. Yeah, of course, its company policy. And I don't do too badly out of it, neither. I pull down £53,000 before tax – even Nick Mephisto can't get round that one. I get a good expense account, commission, company car, and the use of the company health club. Better than being on the dole, I can tell you.'

'What. What do I have to do?' Ambrose heard himself say. He seemed to have no control over his own voice.

'Just sign this,' Morris said, pushing a typewritten contract in front of Ambrose. "Just sign where it's marked, there and there... and there and then initial each page.' and Ambrose found himself with a pen in his hand signing away his soul, almost before he knew what was happening.

'Magic! Magic!' Morris exclaimed, with probably more truth than he realised. 'Big D will be pleased.'

Ambrose shook his head, unable to credit what he had just done.

'What happens now? he asked a little fearfully as reality seeped back into his brain.

'Well, all the paperwork has to go back to Head Office for ratification, once it's approved it'll be passed on to the Technical Department. They carry out the actual assignment, but I should imagine you'll start seeing results by the end of next week. Well, must fly, got another call to make tonight, got to see this MP as wants to be Prime Minister, offering Tory Party souls at a discounted rate. Didn't think they 'ad souls.'

As Ambrose saw Morris out, Mrs. Kubic peered out though her door again. 'Zat you, Mr. Curtain? Your visitor leaving? Goot, I hope he 'as disinfected ze toilet seat.' Then she shut her door again, muttering something about 'perverts' under her breath.

Over the next week Ambrose tried to convince himself that the incident had never happened, that he must have dreamed it, even explaining away the business card from *MEPHISTO UNIVERSAL ENTERPRISES*, telling himself that it must belong to the previous tenants or that it had somehow got stuck to his shoe and he had brought it into his room that way. There had to be some rational explanation. He couldn't possibly have sold his soul to the Devil. Could he?

It was the most horrible dream he had ever had in his entire life. Blood was everywhere, streams of it, buckets of it. On his hands, in his hair, in his mouth. Blood so thick in his mouth he almost choked on it. Everywhere, blood, and through the blood a face floated, a face he knew but could not place, tantalisingly familiar but fading, fading, drowning. Drowning in blood.

Ambrose woke with a start, fighting for breath, drenched in a cold sweat. The bed clothes wringing and twisted, his heart pounding like infernal bellows in his chest. Evan as he lay gasping, the nightmare faded, and all he could remember were visions of blood.

The murder of Ingrid Dobson, the chief accountant at Silver's, was the most terrible shock. She had been attacked on Bayswater Road, close to where she shared a flat with her girlfriend. Her throat was cut and her badly mutilated body dumped across the road in Hyde Park.

The police made hopeful noises but despite massive house to house enquiries, a re-enactment, and television appeals for information, no clues were forthcoming as to the identity of the killer, even though he must have been covered in blood from head to foot.

After a suitable period, Ambrose Curtain was confirmed as chief accountant, although he did feel slightly uneasy about it. Ingrid's death had surely been coincidental but lurking at the back of his mind was the horrible memory of a dream, a dream he had dreamt on the night of the murder.

Ambrose's promotion was duly reported in the Staff Magazine, on the second page next to an announcement that Mildred Barker in Packing had just given birth to her third child. But surely, Ambrose thought, that hardly qualifies as getting your name in the papers, does it? And then he chided himself, telling himself that he had only imagined selling his soul to the 'Big D,' *I must have had too much cheese for supper* but then Ambrose hardly ever ate cheese. *Animal fats are bad for you.*

The night before the second body was found, Ambrose had the dream again, seeing himself awash in blood. As before, he awoke in panic, gasping for breath. What was worse he could not remember where he had been that night. He could remember coming home from the office and cooking a vegetable stir fry but after that nothing, nothing at all until he woke up in a tangle of damp sheets with the phantasm of blood before his eyes.

The dead girl, Miriam Canar, had been attacked near Sussex Square, Bayswater and the manner of her mutilations led the police to believe that it was the same killer who had murdered Ingrid Dobson, but as before, there were no clues as to his identity.

As Ambrose let himself into the hall, Mrs. Kubic poked her head through her door. She waved the 'Evening Standard' at him. 'You see zis, Mr. Curtain? 'Nother poor girl kilt. An' jus' round the corner, too. A body is not safe in her own home.' She sniffed loudly, a sure sign of disapproval. 'You go out again tonight, Mr. Curtain? And las' night you vent out, come back late. I hear you, making ver' big racket, all that water running, running, running. Hope you not been vis dirty girls, bringing back disease?'

'No! No, Mrs Kubic, I was at... the... er... Chess Club. The game went on longer than expected... went down to the... er last pawn. Very tense.'

'Chess? Huh. Filthy perverts, zay play chess!'

Four more dreams, four more bodies, all mutilated the same way, all killed in the Bayswater area. Inevitably it was the 'Sun' newspaper who coined the name 'the Bayswater Butcher,' with a screaming banner headline that read:

'BAYSWATER BUTCHER' STRIKES AGAIN. POLICE BAFFLED.

With each killing, Ambrose could feel his sanity shredding away, distraught as the realisation grew in him that he must be the 'Bayswater Butcher,' he didn't know exactly how but he knew it to be the work of Satan and all pretence that he had not sold his soul vanished as surely as morning mist evaporates in the bright sunlight.

He was unable to concentrate, unable to think of anything other than blood and death. His work began to suffer and the management at Silver's began to look for a replacement chief accountant, convinced that Ambrose was unable to cope with the pressures of his new responsibilities.

He barely ate and was afraid to sleep at night, fearful that the terrible dream would descend upon him, and another girl would die, mortal dread wrapping around him like a black shroud.

Ambrose fought against sleep as long as he could, forcing down cups of thick black coffee in the forlorn hope that the caffeine would keep him awake, even though he knew that too much coffee can be bad for the heart. His eyelids were heavy, thickly coated, and gritty and his head began to nod as waves of exhaustion swept over him. He fought sleep off once more, stabbing himself in the thigh with a fork to keep himself awake, but to no avail and finally he fell asleep in the chair.

The dream was the worst ever; he thought he was drowning. Suffocating in blood. He thrashed and heaved but still the blood rose about his head like a full moon tide. Seven ripped faces swam before his gore-slicked eyes and the face of Ingrid Dodson screamed 'Chief accountant! Chief accountant! Chief accountant! at him as the blood gushed from her slashed throat like a fountain.

'BAYSWATER BUTCHER' CLAIMS VICTIM No 7 'the headlines shouted at Ambrose as he waited to catch the underground train to work. He turned away but all he could see were more headlines as commuters seemed to thrust their newspapers at him in accusation.

Panic swept over him again, his heart pounded fit to burst and he knew he could go on no longer, he knew he could not face another death, another dream. Something had to be done – the killing had to stop.

Mrs. Kubic picked up her copy of the 'Evening Standard' almost before the paper boy had pushed in through the letter box and scurried back to her room.

'BAYSWATER BUTCHER' GIVES HIMSELF UP TO POLICE' ran the lead story. *'Police today confirmed that a thirty-two-year-old man had confessed to the string of murders that has terrorised the Capital.*

A police spokesman said that the suspect had given details of the murders that could only have been known to the killer and that police are satisfied that the main in question is the notorious 'Bayswater Butcher.' A full statement will be issued later'.

'Oh, my Gott,' exclaimed Mrs Kubic as she read the article, clucking in gloating outrage. As she read the rest of the front page another story caught her eye like a polished pebble in black shale.

'London Underground transport came to a halt during rush hour this morning when a man, believed to be suicidal, threw himself under a commuter train at Bayswater Station. The police have identified the victim as Mr. Ambrose Dainty Curtain, aged 32 of 27 Lindburn Street, Bayswater, Enquiries are continuing.'

Ambrose had got his name on the front pages of the newspapers at last.

IF ONLY IT HADN'T BEEN FOR THE FOG

A police station in London. 1978.

The statement lay on the interview room table. Several pages of typed confession. Det Sgt Wallace picked it up and read through it once more.

'It was the taunting that did it. All the time. On at me. Taunting. Laughing. Rubbing my nose in it.'

The interview room was, as always, drab and depressing, the cream and green walls were dirty, the chairs hard, the table brown-stained with tea-cup rings and scorched with cigarette burns, the air over-laden with the smells of guilt, of unwashed bodies, cigarettes, and pine disinfectant that could never, ever, hide the underlying stinks beneath, no matter how liberal the application.

The bobby at the door stared impassively at the opposite walls and Sgt Wallace wondered briefly what was going through his mind – *Last night's football results? Women? The poems of Ezra Pound?* – and then turned to the statement again.

'I didn't really mind about HIM, about the other man. Not as such. I mean, things had got so bad be-

tween Susan and me, so it wasn't that. It was the way she flaunted it. Taunting me with it, saying as how it was better with him than it was with me, you know, better in bed. You get that thrown at you twenty-four hours a day, seven days a week, well, it demeans you. Makes you think less of yourself, less of a person. Unsexes you.'

Curious choice of words, thought Wallace, *unsexes you,* shaking out another cigarette from the packet on the table, lighting it with a match from a box of Swan Vesta, automatically cupping a hand around the flame as though to protect it from a high wind and then took a deep drag, the smoke rattling harshly at the back of the throat.

'Any chance of a cup of tea?' Wallace asked, picking up the typewritten sheets again. 'Dry work, is this.'

'I can't say exactly when I decided to kill them, I mean, it doesn't come to you in a flash, like lightning or a divine revelation does it? It grows on you. Slowly. Undetected. Like cancer. Malignant. Then one day, it's there, full grown and it's as if you've known all along. I even knew then how I was going to do it. And when. It was all laid out before me. You see, I wanted to catch them together. In bed. So they could see it in my eyes and know that they were going to die. And know that it was me killing them. I had to see it, you see? I had to smell their fear. Taste it, taste it on my tongue, like a viper.

After only a few puffs, the cigarette joined the

others in the ashtray, the ashtray already overflowing with mangled dog-ends, spent matches and ash.

'I had to go to Glasgow for the conference and I knew that as soon as I was out of the door, as soon as I was on my way to the airport, HE would be round. So that's when I decided to do it, during the conference. Make sure that I was seen in Glasgow and that would be my alibi, nobody would question it. As long as I was in Glasgow and registered for the conference, as long as I was seen at the opening address and the welcome dinner and was there for the second day, the final day, nobody would know. I mean, these conferences are so big, hundreds of delegates from all over the country and I knew I would not be missed. So long as I was back in the hotel for breakfast and the morning session, none would ever question it, would they, I would have to make sure the bed looked slept in but that was no problem. Easy!'

The tea, when it came, was hot and sweet, but with a thin slick of bubbly grease floating on top, the milk had obviously started to go off and after a few sips, it was allowed to go cold.

'The opening address and the welcoming session began at 7:30 in the evening, after registration, to be followed by a reception with cocktails and then dinner. The first working session did not begin until 10:00 the next morning.

I caught the shuttle flight to Glasgow that afternoon, the 17th, the 7th February and checked in at the hotel, the same hotel where the conference was held, I think most of the delegates would have been staying there.

Before I left the house, I unfastened the window locks and replaced the screws with smaller ones, screws that barely held the locks in place. It looked as though the windows were locked and unless you actually rattled the windows hard you would never know. All I had to do was slip a knife in the crack of the window frame and the window could easily be forced open. I got the idea from a television programme. I can't remember what it is called, it's the one with the female detective who gets no help from her male colleagues but still manages to solve the case.

I couldn't use my door key, you see, she's have had all the security chains and bolts fastened.

The young constable at the door shuffled his feet and suddenly popped his knuckles, the bony *CRACK* sounding loudly round the still bare room. Sgt Wallace looked up in distraction before reading on.

She was gloating again as I left, Susan I mean, I could see it in her eyes, taunting. I could have killed her then, easily, but I wanted them both, do you see? No justification for it else, just the one.

Anyway, as I said, I flew up to Glasgow, checked in, went to the reception, and made sure that I was seen, spoke to people and then went to the dinner. I can't remember what we had to eat, mind on other things you see, savouring the look in their eyes when they knew I was going to kill them, but I had a good appetite, I do remember that!

SOMETIMES YOU JUST KILL THE WRONG PEOPLE

. . .

Chair legs scraped on the scuffed vinyl floor tiles as Wallace leaned back in the hard plastic chair, easing knotted back muscles, arms stretched out tight, fingers hooked together tautly.

I caught the overnight train from Glasgow, there being no flights at night. I intended to sleep on the train, but I wasn't able to. I felt too excited, I guess, too... righteous to sleep. I didn't go in for disguise at all, no wigs or glasses, nothing silly like that, but I did wear a hat, pulled down low so I wouldn't be recognised on the CCTV. You can't be too sure, can you? It was still dark, not yet daybreak, when the train pulled into the station where I had left my car. I dropped it off there on the way to the airport and took the tube the rest of the way.

It was very quiet, barely light, when I parked the car in the street next to mine. Apart from a milk float in the distance the street was deserted, not a soul around. I felt as though I were the only person alive on earth, apart from THEM, that is and that wasn't going to last much longer.

I put on rubber gloves when I got to my house, for fingerprints on the window, you know, just in case. Silly really, why shouldn't my fingerprints be there, it's my house? The knife slipped easily into the frame and with hardly any effort the window swung open, although the knife did make a mark in the paintwork, and I wasn't expecting that.

The house was very quiet, still, waiting for me. I

know that sounds fanciful but that's exactly how it felt, as though somehow it knew what I was going to do. And approved.

The big knife was in the kitchen drawer. It's a chef's knife, very sharp, very long, we use it for cutting meat and that is exactly what I was going to use it for. To cut meat. Rotten meat.

I took off my shoes and all my clothes down to my underwear. The kitchen floor felt cold on my feet, I remember that, very cold. Then I crept upstairs to the bedroom.

I had to kill him first and quickly because otherwise he would fight and struggle. I opened the door slowly and there they were. In bed. He was in MY place, on MY side of the bed. I always sleep on the right-hand side of the bed. Always. The bastard was snoring, snoring like the pig he was.

I put the blade to his throat and with my other hand I pulled back the covers and shook him. He came awake slowly, grunting 'What? What?' Then he saw me and felt the knife at his throat. I could see the fear on him, smell it in his pores and then I cut his throat. SWISH. Just like that. SWISH. So easy, like slicing cucumber. She awoke then and saw me and saw the blood and began to scream. So, I leaned over and stabbed her in the chest, across her dirty breasts, into her foul heart, maybe not the first cut but one of them. Then I slashed her lying face, stabbed out those taunting eyes. She'll taunt me no longer.

The door to the Interview Room opened and Inspector Lomax came. He took a chair next to Sgt Wallace who looked up briefly and then carried on reading.

SOMETIMES YOU JUST KILL THE WRONG PEOPLE

. . .

I never knew there could be so much blood, I ought to have done, I suppose, but it's different when it's fresh like that. So much blood.

I checked again which side the cut on his throat ran from, it ran from his left to the right, so I closed his right-hand over the knife handle, wanted it to look like a lover's quarrel, as if he had killed her and then cut his own throat in remorse.

I showered then, washed it all away, letting the taps run a long time.

Then, I ran downstairs, dressed, replaced the proper screws in the window, bundled myself up in my hat and coat and let myself out through the front door, locked it behind me and walked to my car. Walked normally, no haste. Nothing attracts people's attention like haste, so I made myself walk slowly. I drove back to the airport and caught the morning shuttle flight back to Glasgow.

I think you know the rest. There was fog at Glasgow Airport and we diverted to Edinburgh. I still had things under control, but the only way y I could get back to Glasgow quickly was to hire a car, if I had waited for the airline coach I'd still be there now. But of course, I had to hire the car in my own name, show my driving license, use my credit card, that was the only record of my presence anywhere. I mean, the 'plane ticket was bought for cash using a false name. If it hadn't been for the fog no-one would ever have been able to trace me.

I got lost coming through Glasgow, all those one-way systems. I ended up miles away from the hotel and by the time I found my way back it had long gone past lunchtime. And by then of course, you were waiting for me. Not you personally but other officers. They were there to tell me about Susan and HIM, how their bodies had been found. They SHOULDN'T have been found so soon, I mean, the idea was that I should find them when I got back from the conference and could prove that I had been in Glasgow all the time.

But the window-cleaner was a peeping tom. He ought to be locked away, peering through the gaps in people's curtains like that. Disgusting! Some people have no sense of decency, do they? Anyway, peering through the windows like the pervert he is, he saw the bodies and called the police.

And so there they were. Looking for me in Glasgow, knowing I was supposed to be at the conference, everybody knew I was supposed to be at the conference, that was the whole point! They were very suspicious by then and very hostile when they started to question me. What about the hire car? Where had I been? I said for a drive. Of course, they checked the details of the hire and found I had picked up the car at Edinburgh airport. What was I doing at Edinburgh airport when I was supposed to be in Glasgow, and it didn't take long for them to find out about the diverted flight and put two and two together. And then two of the airline crew identified me as a passenger. After that there didn't seem much point in denying it. I mean, it's not as though I had done anything wrong, was it, THEY were the ones in the wrong. Flaunting it like that all the time.

If only it hadn't been for the fog, everything would have been perfect.

Wallace finished reading and passed the statement to Inspector Lomax who quickly leafed through the pages and then reached inside his jacket pocket and handed a pen to the killer to sign it.

Det. Sgt Julia Wallace took the pen and in a small, neat hand signed and initialled her confession.

If only it hadn't been for the fog.

THE END

For a more whimsical read, Giles Ekins has written another volume of stories of a more general genre, including the prize-winning story 'Back to Basics' historical stories such as 'Portents,' 'Shadows of a Dream' and 'The Lemonade Stall,' the comedic 'Call Me Ruby' as well as a heart-breaking love story, 'And in the Shimmering Light of Dawn,' bound to bring tears to the eye.

'Back to Basics and Other Stories' is published by Next Chapter Publishing and is available in all formats.

Dear reader,

We hope you enjoyed reading *Sometimes You Just Kill The Wrong People*. Please take a moment to leave a review, even if it's a short one. Your opinion is important to us.

Discover more books by Giles Ekins at
https://www.nextchapter.pub/authors/giles-ekins

Want to know when one of our books is free or discounted? Join the newsletter at
http://eepurl.com/bqqB3H

Best regards,
Giles Ekins and the Next Chapter Team

ABOUT THE AUTHOR

Giles Ekins was born in the North East of England and qualified as an Architect in London. Subsequently he spent many years living and working in Northern Nigeria, Qatar, Oman, and Bahrain working on the design and construction of various projects including schools, hospitals, leisure centres, Royal palaces, shopping malls, and most particularly highly prestigious hotels.

He has now returned to England and lives in Sheffield with his wife Patricia. Amongst other works, Giles is the author of 'Sinistrari' 'Murder by Illusion' 'Gallows Walk' Dead Girl Found' and the children's book 'The Adventures of a Travelling Cat,' all published by Next Chapter Books.

Sometimes You Just Kill The Wrong People
ISBN: 978-4-86747-506-5
Mass Market

Published by
Next Chapter
1-60-20 Minami-Otsuka
170-0005 Toshima-Ku, Tokyo
+818035793528

19th May 2021

www.ingramcontent.com/pod-product-compliance
Lightning Source LLC
LaVergne TN
LVHW032010070526
838202LV00059B/6381